SECRET SHADOWS

SECRET SHADOWS

ALEXA WHITEWOLF

Secret Shadows
An Immortal Rogues Novel

by Alexa Whitewolf
Copyright ©2020 Alexa Whitewolf

Cover design by Y. Nikolova at **Ammonia Book Covers**

Kindle First Edition
ASIN: B08KSSJ4M6

Author's Note & Acknowledgements

Mythology has been my "fix". While most kids were growing up playing in mud (I did that, too), I dug my nose in books. One of the first books I remember reading is Legends of Olympus. It was by a Romanian author and had a compilation of Greek mythology stories about Zeus, Hera, Poseidon, Apollo, Artemis, etc. It was a great read, and stuck with me. My worn copies now have a special place on my bookshelves, along with my Ancient Egypt mythology books and others. Needless to say, mythology became a big passion.

And when I started writing paranormal romance, it was a natural segue. *Moonlight Rogues* was my first full paranormal romance series, tracking wolves from different backgrounds and mythologies. When I finished the series at the end of 2019, I knew I wasn't done with it. It has now progressed into an entire universe. Amelia, one of my readers, one day suggested Rogues Extended Universe as a potential name and it stuck. So within that universe… Well, I'll include the reading order a bit later.

Know that *Immortal Rogues* **can** be read without having read the rest of the series. *Flaming Rogues* does have some of the characters, but they're secondary in here.

Last, if you prefer your gods perfect and your goddesses demure, you may want to skip this one. These gods are raw, and edgy, and very human. That's why we like them 😊

Huge thanks to my family for sticking by me. I had originally promised my husband to be done with writing for the year when this idea hit and hooked, andddd that led to a few extra weeks of "cave writing."

Huge thanks to Siobhan for your amazing beta comments and for keeping me in line! To all the bloggers and readers supporting this universe, you guys rock!

Happy readings,

Alexa 😊

Rogues Extended Universe – Reading Order

Quick Glossary

Not as much Romanian in here as you've come to expect with the Rogues, but! Since Ileana and Făt-Frumos show up, I thought it only fair to mention there are *some* words.

Da/nu – Yes/no

Mda – mmyeah

Parteneră – partner (fem.)

Draga mea – my darling (fem.)

Zmei – dragon shifters (plural; sing. zmeu)

And the names…

Ileana – pronounced E-lya-nah

Făt-Frumos – pronounced Fuh-th Fruh-mohs

*These last two are heroes of lore in Romanian folklore 😊

The destiny of man is in his own soul.

Herodotus

PROLOGUE

The room was, by all accounts, luxurious. Thick, plushy carpets, golden goblets strewn about, velvet couches. And off to the side, the largest wall was, in fact, no wall at all. Instead, it was a massive wheel. Held together by golden parts, it spun and spun its threads, which were split between three other wheels, much smaller. They were part of a trio of spinning wheels, and were set at the three corners of the room, awaiting their mistresses.

"Clotho!"

A raven-haired woman in a silky white toga entered the room, weaving her long locks into a braid. "Yes, yes. I'm here already, Atropos."

Her sister, with equally dark hair but a lavender toga, rolled her eyes. They each had sharp, almost bird-like features, with large noses and thin lips. It was an odd sort of beauty, common enough in their realm, and shunned outside of it.

"Late as always." A third person rose from a velvet couch.

"You're one to talk, Lachesis," the one called Clotho said. "And may I remind you this was your idea?"

The three sisters converged in the center of the room. Their features displayed amusement and boredom in equal measure.

Lachesis sipped from a dark goblet, ran a hand through her messy hair, and said, "And you both agreed. It is time we stop being simple watchers of the mess unfolding and start creating solutions."

"I thought the immortal race we created *was* the solution," Atropos muttered. "That's what you said back then."

Lachesis pouted. "I thought so, too. They were promising, more inflexible than the zmei. Dragon shifters and strong those may be, but diplomatic they are most definitely not. But, alas, even immortals have their drawbacks."

"They've only been around a few hundred years, Lach. Give them a chance."

"The problem is we have no time for chances. Only way we can stop what we have all seen is by taking charge."

"Is it proper, though? To start messing about with the destinies of the gods themselves?" Clotho asked.

Lachesis shrugged. "It is no more than they do with humans. And it is about time they have a taste of powerlessness."

Atropos drank the last of her nectar and tossed the cup to the side, then headed to one of the less imposing spinning wheels. The thread being spun automatically was the same color as her brown toga, whereas Clotho's was white, and Lachesis' was lavender.

"Who do we begin with?" Atropos asked.

Clotho and Lachesis each took their places as well, reaching their hands over their own instruments.

"Zeus," Lachesis said. "Let us give him a woman who will make his life hell."

"Oooh!" Clotho chuckled. "And let us do Hades next. I feel bad, being the cause of his little unfortunate situation so long ago."

"You *were* rather drunk when he was created. If you hadn't messed with his thread…"

Clotho shrugged. "It is for the best, no? Being perfect is such a chore. He's much more interesting these days." She gazed into the thread, picturing the moody god. "Perhaps giving him a mate who'll quiet the chaos in his mind will help."

Laughter rose all around, then the sisters got to work. Their nimble fingers spun the wheels and played with the threads, as more and more magic emerged from their fingertips in star-like dust.

And so the fates of the gods were forever changed once more…

CHAPTER ONE

One step, two steps, three steps—fuck.

I take a swig of the realm-renowned ambrosia from my cup, then try to catch my balance. After all, a precarious walk on my brother's roof isn't the best spot for someone like me to be.

Zeus is probably out frolicking again. Why would I ever choose to marry that womanizer? Father must be crazy. Hera. Goddess of marriage and birth, soon to be queen of Olympus.

I peek below, not seeing her. Of course not. Because if I could see her, it would mean I'm perfectly sane. And simply hearing her regular cursing as she's being pushed toward a future she has no desire for. It would have nothing to do with the real reason for what I'm picking up on.

I wonder what it'll take for Apollo to notice me.

This time, the wishful thinking emanates from a nymph. Her long, curly white hair dances as she sprints across the golden path below me. *Far* below me.

It, much like this new mausoleum of a building, has replaced our previous version of Olympus. Gone are the woods and rivers I'd grown used to, where I could seek out peace. Instead, we have a type of palace built in bold contrasts of light and dark stone, with windows twice my size and furnishings that would make an emperor jealous…

Zeus keeps saying it's where human architecture is heading into the future, but who am I to say? They've only just developed their own tribes and customs. They're such a young species, compared to us… Then again, my brother has better mastery of the oracles than I do.

Through blurry eyes, I squint at the nymph.

She disappears farther into the manicured gardens. Gardens I have a perfect view of, not that it matters. Last thing I want is to see more of Apollo's conquests.

He's everything I wished I was. Charming, carefree, a master of archery, music, seduction, poetry, you name it. Who *wouldn't* want to fuck him?

Besides me, that is.

I take another swig from the cup. The amber liquid burns down my throat, less and less appealing, its honeyed sweetness almost enough to make me sick. But it serves to keep my senses dull, if only for the moment.

If Father thinks I'm going through with this sham—so, what, Zeus can fuck anything that moves and constantly humiliate me? Hera, again.

It's been a while since Olympus had another party. Some other god, probably within the vicinity.

One would think those are memories, only they're not. They're thoughts, and thanks to some laugh of the Fates I can't pinpoint, I've been cursed to hear them. *All* of them. Day in and day out, night in and night out. Without a break. Ever.

When further nectar runs down my throat, my balance becomes even more off. Drunkenness doesn't last long, which is why I always have to refill my cup. But for the time it does imbue my spirit, and, well…it sure is fun.

I make a show of putting one foot in front of the other, swaying treacherously over the edge. A quick glance down tells me there's nothing underneath me except the marble pathway intertwined with golden whorls. Zeus went all out in this new creation; white-and-dark marble combines with liquid gold threading through the stone, like many lightning bolts.

He's not yet ruler of this land. But he wants to be. Oh, how he wants to be.

The floors seem all the more appealing, given they would shut off my brain. At least temporarily. *Hmm. Tempting.*

Gods cannot die, thus I'm not afraid of a little fall. But we can get injured, even if those injuries get healed within moments. I'm sure a teensy fall won't be too hard, but it might give me a break from these *voices.*

"Hades!"

I stop mid-gulp and glance around. It

takes a moment for my blurry gaze to focus.

My brother, the blond giant, glares at me. He's standing in the midst of the courtyard, having just emerged from the gardens. Part of me wonders if he frolicked with the nymph while he was there, but then I shrug it off. Not my business. Hasn't been for a while.

Those blue eyes used to smile with mischief in our youth. Before he found out. Before he made his own judgment on what I am. Before I became...lesser...in his eyes.

"Zeus-y boy!" I take another gulp, then when the cup is empty, I wave my hand over it to refill it. I raise it toward him, and some of the liquid sloshes over the brim. I wave heartily with my free hand, looking every bit the jester, knowing it'll only annoy him more.

Oh, how right I am.

"Get down!" he shouts, stepping toward me. *Of all the times for him to make a spectacle of himself, it has to be this week?* "Before someone sees you."

"Why?"

For a moment, he only blinks. "What do you mean, why? Because I've had it with your acting out." *And I'm so damned tired of*

living in constant fear someone'll find out all the
shit you can do. That you can outwit us all.

I take another swig, ignoring him. I could, indeed, head down. Jump off, or simply walk back inside the mansion—current iteration of Olympus 3.0—and listen. But then, that would be boring. And as everyone knows, I'm anything but boring.

Zeus' eyes shine, then a bolt of lightning hits where I'm next stepping. I arch an eyebrow toward him and receive another glare. Behind him, a few gods have caught on to the exchange. Their thoughts are getting louder.

Hades, again. Why am I not surprised?

If Zeus doesn't get him in hand soon, how's he supposed to rule over us? After all, he needs to show he can clean his own house first before taking over Olympus.

Such a disgrace. I'd expect this from Bacchus, not from a prince.

I rub the sides of my temples, then make a fist and hurl it against my skull repeatedly. "Shut up! Everyone, just shut the fuck up! For once in your miserable existences—"

Zeus zaps me again, cutting me off. The bolt of lightning hits me in the stomach, and I fly over the archway of the mansion, landing a few feet from him with a grunt. Something must've broken, at some point. But by the time I raise my head, I'm already better.

Except for the fact my ambrosia cup is empty yet again. Zeus stomps to me and kicks it away, then looms over me.

"Are you about done, now?" Zeus says, loud enough for everyone else to hear. Then he steps closer, lowering his voice. "I have had it with your actions. If you don't soon learn to step in line, we'll have an issue." *And I may have to take more permanent actions to keep you in check.*

Funny. Normally he's so careful with his thoughts around me. Today, he's more off his game than I am.

I get up, not bothering to hide my scoff as I dust myself off. "We already have an issue, *brother*."

Before he can stop me, I walk away in search of more oblivion.

Dawn comes and goes, and I blink awake next in the middle of day. Someone's banging on my door. I push the warm, pliant body of a nymph—whatever her name is—to the side and move off the bed. The knocking only increases.

I stifle as a yawn as I open the door. "Yes?"

Pegasus rolls his eyes. "You could at least put some clothes on."

My best friend since I saved him from a Kraken—yes, there are more than one of the mythical monsters of the seas—he also keeps me in line. More than once, he's saved me from doing something stupid, though that's becoming harder and harder these days.

If there's anyone in Olympus undeserving of my scorn, it's Pegasus. So I shrug and let him in while heading to get dressed.

Most humans would see him as a flying, white horse. He is, of course—if he so decides. We can all choose our forms, and most of us stick with the human one we've been in for eons. It beats floating around like essences of air, fire or lightning, after all. Our true forms, for those of us who remember.

I pull on some clothes and shoo the

nymph away, then face Pegasus. We could be brothers, with our dark hair. Only he wears his longer, and he's bulkier than me, closer to Zeus' shape.

"What brings you here?" I ask.

After all, it's not every day he comes to visit me. My quarters in the mansion are not to his liking, one could say. While most Olympians choose to stay in this massive hotel—my brother's great idea—they also go crazy with décor. In particular, Hera much prefers her area in old Persian colors, while Zeus himself loves weather-themed décor. Not surprising.

For myself? I glance around, taking in the dark colors, the ancient feel. I spend so much time hiding in here, you'd think I would've done more with the place. Especially given I've had eons to do so.

Oh, well.

"Many, many things." Pegasus plops down on an antique, black leather chair. "Rumor has it you caused another scene?"

"Mm."

Ah, friend, if only I knew what troubles you...

I try to pretend I didn't hear that particular

thought. It's getting worse these days, but at least there's only us two in here now that the nymph is gone. "It happens," I say instead. "Zeus pushes all my wrong buttons."

"And you don't push his?"

I sip from another ambrosia cup, refusing to dignify that with an answer.

"Come now, Hades. Zeus is asserting his hold on Olympus. The Council looks for fault in everything he does, even though we all know they're a bunch of old and prickly deities."

Why does he have to be so reasonable?

"And still, they have power."

Pegasus shrugs at my tone. "Too much. But at least they keep the pantheons from killing each other."

Ah, yes. The ever-present struggle of *us*.

It's a good thing humans don't realize how close to annihilation they came. Our incessant fighting was horrid, to the point we had to split the world into various geographical areas, each governed by one pantheon. Olympians got Greece and its surroundings, Celts got the upper lands, and… Well, you can figure out the rest. A Council comprised of each pantheon's representatives was set to oversee it all, and to ensure any disagreements are brought to them for, hmm, *diplomatic* solutions.

Of course, Olympus already has its own conclave on top of that, made up of my brother, some older gods, and plenty of stuffiness to go with it. It's this same panel Zeus is trying to wrench Olympus from, to remake it to his own image.

Sometimes I wonder if out of the three of us, he got all the ambition.

I peek inside my goblet, scowling as if my bad mood is the liquor's fault. Is it just me or has the nectar stopped working? "It's not like anyone forced us to retire from the world of humans."

"No, but can you deny it was the best thing?"

My only answer is another shrug. I don't really know. When the choice was made, I was still struggling with the voices. With being different. Weakness is not a trait understood in Olympus, especially when you're a crown prince like me, Zeus, and Poseidon. And yet…

"Probably." I swirl the cup and take a bigger gulp.

When the gods chose retirement, they each went to their own pantheons. The Celts, the Norse, the Egyptians—we've all stopped talking to one another. In a way, perhaps it's best. But sometimes, I wonder.

When the dreams wake me in the middle of the night, with nightmares I cannot understand nor want to, I wonder. This feeling that something is coming…

Wherever does his mind go in times like these?

I roll my shoulders and force a grin at Pegasus. It wouldn't do to have him analysing me too closely. "Enough about the politics of our world. Why are you really here?"

He smirks. Seems my best friend has gotten just as good as me at masking his worries. "Thought you'd want the latest gossip."

"Gossip?"

"Mm. They've gotten us guards."

"Us? Who's us?"

"Not sure yet." Pegasus taps the side of the armchair, glancing around himself. "Is this new?" When I shake my head, he grunts. "Why do I even bother asking? I don't understand why out of all of us, you choose such scrappy décor. Anyway. Give me a cup, would you?"

I snap my fingers, and a similar goblet to mine materializes in his hand. Soon, it fills with ambrosia. That's the benefit of this land—you ask, and you receive. Or, in our case, we *think it* and it *materializes*.

Pegasus glances within, takes a whiff, and smiles. "Zeus' special reserve again?"

I shrug. "He won't mind."

"I very much doubt that." He takes a sip and sighs in satisfaction. "But wow, is it good." *If only he'd drink less, maybe there would be hope for their brotherly bond. I've never understood what broke them apart such.*

And you never will. I bite the words back. "You were saying? The gossip?"

"Ah, right. Well, rumors have been around for ages of an immortal school. Do you not remember the whole debacle with the zmei, a while back?"

I think back on it. Zeus did mention something about a pet project gone wrong. But was it only centuries, or millennia ago? It's getting rather hard to keep track of it.

"Was it those dragon shifters, in the Carpathians?"

Pegasus nods. "The same ones. Apparently, the Council decided they were useless, after all. Too full of raw emotions. So, they've created another race, one more likely to serve us as they are supposed to."

"Uh-huh…"

"They're calling them immortals—beings of pure light."

"I'm still waiting for the punch line."

"Thought you'd want to check out their graduation with me? Their training has just ended and some are about to receive their assignments."

I snort. "Pass, but thank you." Somehow, making myself more visible around other creatures, and losing my shit at their inner voices again, doesn't seem appealing. Zeus may not forgive me this soon after the last time.

When I head to the door, Pegasus calls out. "Where are you off to, then?"

"Somewhere much more fun."

CHAPTER TWO

The music is loud, the laughter even more so, and still, I stick to the shadows. No one else gets it, my attraction to humans. They think it's a whim. Zeus can go and fuck everything that moves in the mortal world, but I show an interest? Then it's the new coming of the apocalypse.

"Hiya, handsome."

The girl's slurring her words, but it doesn't take away from her prettiness. Curly blonde waves, light hazel eyes, and a pouty mouth. Her well-endowed bosom plays hide and seek with me as she giggles and moves to the beat of drums and flutes. Clearly old enough to play around.

"Hello, yourself."

She giggles again and moves closer, grabbing my hands and yanking me to my feet. I let the music and her warm body help me forget everything. After all, that's why I come to the humans—even if I have no idea where I've ended up right now.

Time passes, and still we sway. The upbeat tunes of some instrument or another keep my mind busy, or perhaps it's a result of the drink I don't let go of. The faint torches around us spin and spin, and the girl's thoughts assail me. *Bet he'd be good in bed... My gosh, that mouth...* And so on.

Does it stroke my ego? Sure. None of the goddesses back home will give me the time of day, unless it's to solicit favors from Zeus. Partly because they think me crazy, and partly because my personality isn't sunny enough. In Olympus, that's not something to be sought out. Here, I'm always the center of attention. Who wouldn't keep returning?

I smile at the girl, letting my hands roam over her lower back, pulling her closer. I dip my head, whispering sweet nothings in her ear, trying to ignore the thoughts all around me… And I become aware of something else.

Someone watching.

My body goes rigid as I scan the surroundings. Nothing. Only drunken humans, more ale, and girls too tipsy to count. And yet…

In the distance, a flash of dark hair catches my eye. A low, female laugh. A coy look. And just like that, my interest in the human wanes, and I move away. She begs me to stay, holding my hand, but I hear nothing—oddly, even the music has stopped. Or is it just in my mind?

I follow past the throng of humans, the sounds of drunken behavior, and around darkened houses. The time has not yet come for these humans to know more than firelight…but perhaps it will. A few centuries from now.

Where did she go?

I'd only caught a glimpse, it's not even like her appearance attracted me. I didn't see much of her. But there was something else, underneath it. As fast as I saw her, a darkness lingered around her.

Maybe I really am losing my mind.

No matter where I search for her, I can't find her. Whoever she was…

Dejected, I prepare to leave. To return to the party. Only, I realize I'm far away from the mortals, farther than I should be. Woods are nearby, and there is no glint from the moon, hidden behind trees. And while the music lures me closer, a different kind of sound stops me. A growl, in the dead of the night.

This time, my movements are more cautious, careful. I pivot toward it.

All I see are eyes glinting in the darkness, fur, canines… It jumps to attack me. And it—whatever the fuck *it* is—is massive. His paws, five times the size of my hands, grab on to my shoulders and push me to the ground.

His claws dig in my flesh, and his enormous jaw opens, as if ready to swallow me whole. The sharp canines should distract me, but the wounds in his mouth grab my attention. They look…almost as if he's been stabbed by a sword.

And then it hits me. Pegasus' incessant gossiping, a few hundred years ago. "Fenrir?"

I should be tossing him off me, using my deity magic. If nothing else, I'd be a fair match. But this isn't just any wolf, nor does any of this make sense.

Fenrir belongs to the Norse gods. And long ago—not sure how long exactly since my memory tends to be fuzzy these days—he rebelled against Odin, the head of the pantheon, and some others. I'd heard something about him biting off a god's arm and being unwilling to release him until they tricked him with a sword in his mouth.

Was that really only a few centuries ago?

The wolf pants in my face, his breath putrid, and then his head moves, one red eye catching mine. Whatever's in his mind... The connection is enough. An outpour of his thoughts drips into me. *Pain. Agony. Need...need...*

"Need what?" I whisper, gritting my teeth. I can't make myself hurt him. Even if he's about to kill me. Perhaps it would be best that way, putting me out of my misery.

"Enough!"

A flash of something bursts, and Fenrir is tossed off me. Then someone stands between us. He's lean, and his staff is pointing to the— yeah, definitely wolf. There's not much light, but it's enough to see it. With a growl and a whine, he's gone, disappearing into a black, blurry portal.

The newcomer faces me, arching an eyebrow. "Bored again, Hades?"

"You would know, Hermes of the Winged Feet."

Herald and messenger of Olympus, he's also a thorn in my side and a supporter of Zeus. Then again, who isn't? By default, that makes me a thorn in *his* side, and a wild card.

Hermes scowls, adjusting his grip on his staff. The white-winged roman sandals that gave him his name flutter near the ground. He never did like that nickname, but it stuck thanks to the right people sharing it around.

"It's high time you return to Olympus."

Not one of my fans, this one.

"Thanks, but Zeus doesn't need me there. And besides, I'm not done here. Not yet, anyway."

"It wasn't a request, Hades. You've caused enough trouble."

And not for the first time. Why your brother keeps you around instead of exiling you is beyond me.

Ouch. I ignore his thought and instead force a smile. "Zeus causes more messes than me every time he visits the humans."

"But Zeus knows how to stay out of trouble!"

"Sure, he does," I mutter. "How about you tell me what that thing was, then go on your merry way? I'll take care of myself."

Hermes only stares, more than annoyed. His mental swearing would make Zeus blush. I pretend not to catch a single word. And right as he opens his mouth to yell some more, someone else appears, materializing from a cloud of white fog—Pegasus.

He drinks from a cup and burps loudly, then slaps a hand over Hermes' back. He promptly heads to me next. "So this is where you were hiding!"

"How did you know?"

"Followed old Hermes here. Heard grumblings you'd gotten into trouble again."

"I didn't."

"Mm. Hermes, be a dear and let the big boys run amuck. I'll make sure to bring Hades back before his curfew."

My brother's messenger stares at me. I wince at his piercing gaze.

"It would do you well if Fenrir *had* marked you, foolish Hades, instead of simply attacking." A moment later, he's gone, disappeared in a puff of white smoke.

Pegasus is quiet for a moment, but when he faces me there's no laughter in his eyes. "Fenrir? As in, demon dog of the Norse mythology?"

"Yeah, yeah, same one." I turn to leave, but he grabs my arm.

"Hades. Talk to me." *What the hell would Fenrir be doing here? Why attack Hades?*

It's hard to ignore his thoughts, at the same time trying to focus on my own. And much of the same questions swirl in my mind. "I don't know what to say. I followed a girl here, and then Fenrir popped out. Seemed ready to take a bite out of me."

Pegasus lets me go, his jaw going slack. "You have to tell Zeus."

"Why? Wouldn't be the first time the pantheons got their shit crossed over something or other. Zeus probably slept with someone he wasn't supposed to, and Fenrir wants to return the favor."

"Hades… Fenrir is supposed to be imprisoned. Or don't you recall me saying he bit a god's hand off?"

"I do." I rub my chin, then shrug. "Still don't see how it affects me."

"Because his own pantheon wants him locked up! At the very least, Odin and the rest need to be warned he's free. Which is why you need to tell Zeus."

"I'm sure Hermes will take care of that."

"Hades—"

I roll my eyes. "Can we please have some fun?"

Pegasus purses his lips. *If this is important enough, and he gets hurt in the process, I won't ever forgive myself.*

It feels wrong, hearing his thoughts, and his worry softens my heart. I may not be able to admit to understanding his concern, but at least I can ease it a tad.

"I'll tell Zeus next time I see him, all right?"

Pegasus grins at my reluctant mutter and claps me on the shoulder. "Perfect! That'll do. And yes, we can go have fun now."

But right as we're about to leave, we are interrupted once more. Only this time, it's by a woman. She appears out of nowhere, glances around, and then her gaze lands on me. Long brown hair cascades to her waist, her robe is made of multi-colored flowers, and the scent of cinnamon permeates the air around her. Her eyes shine like the sun at dusk, and I find myself rooted to the ground.

Pegasus recovers first. "And where did you come from, darling?"

She does something that could pass for a smile, then flicks her hand at him and my friend is immobilized. The shock in his mind rouses me from my stupor.

"What did you —?"

"Hades, I take it?" She's cool as a cucumber in her inspection of me. "Your brother sent me. This realm is not safe for you, and I am to bring you home."

I cross my arms over my chest. "Uh-huh. And, who are you?"

"My name is Ileana Cosânzeana. You will not have heard of me, but your reputation precedes you."

I chuckle, going for my most charming smile. "I see. And which pantheon do you belong to? For my brother to have roped you into babysitting duties, surely you owe him a favor."

"No favor. No pantheon. I am not of your kin."

"No? And what are you, then?"

"An immortal. Now, I take it you are ready to return home? I made arrangements."

The assurance in her tone rankles me the wrong way. What's going on here, exactly? "And I would follow, why?"

"Whoever said anything about follow?"

Before I can argue, she waves her hand, and a portal appears behind her. With a wintry smile my way, she grabs hold of my shirt and drags me within its pale, swirly depths.

CHAPTER THREE

"What the *fuck*!"

I emerge out of the vortex, spitting and spluttering, less the image of a god than of a surly human. Whirling on the immortal, I jab my index in her face. "Who do you think you are?"

"Your guard." *Mda, typical. Of course, I had to get the childish one.*

I ignore her thoughts and the snark so unlike the image she projects. Looking at her, she's a head smaller than me, tiny in comparison. How, exactly, is she supposed to protect me?

Never mind that. It's probably bad she

doesn't seem even mildly impressed with my angry tone. I don't like this lack of control, this sudden babysitter that's been thrust upon me.

Since I can't acknowledge her thoughts out loud, I settle for, "I don't *need* a guard!"

"Then you should tell your brother, not me."

I storm off, but her footsteps echo behind me. Clearly, she's taking this new assignment to heart. What had Pegasus said about immortals and guards? I should've paid more attention. *Argh.* And whatever the hell Zeus is playing at, I've no idea. But I will get to the bottom of this.

With each stomp of my foot, my power releases in bursts. We pass a hall of mirrors, and only cracks are left in my path. The woman—Ileana—mutters something behind me, but my blood is pounding too hard in my ears to listen.

Determined to get myself heard by Zeus, I make my way through the mansion and into his quarters. Gold and marble tones surround everything, extending over two floors. But he is nowhere to be found.

So I trample over to the next place—Hera's.

And still, Ileana follows me around like my damned shadow.

"Hera!" I roar once I enter her chambers, only some feet away from Zeus'.

A tub has been placed by the window, and she's soaking in it. The scent of roses and jasmine comes to my nose, then surrounds me.

I glare at her. "I'm not in the mood for your games." Or to be suffocated by her perfume.

Hera steps out of her bath, unashamed of her nudity. She takes in my angry expression, then glances behind me.

"Ah. I see you found your new pet."

"More like she found me." I take a step closer. "What is this, Hera? What's Zeus playing at?"

She shrugs and dons a robe. "Only he knows. My guess? Keeping you out of trouble so he can take over Olympus."

She's nothing if not blunt, this one.

"Where is he?"

"You'd know better than me."

I narrow my eyes on her. Whatever the

implication, I don't have the time nor the patience for it. Yet another reason I wish to leave Olympus. And I would tomorrow, if I could. "Tell him I want to speak to him as soon as he's back."

If he's in the mood, I will.

I ignore her thoughts, instead exiting the room and slamming the door behind me. Judging by the presence at my back, I've yet to get rid of my so-called guard.

Ileana follows me into my sleeping quarters, and that's where I draw the line. I turn on her, catching her by surprise as she nearly collides with me. Her cinnamon scent fills my nostrils, and staring into those eyes, I forget for a moment what I'd meant to say.

And then it comes back to me, and I push away all other thoughts. Leave it to Zeus to pick a pretty guard, but that doesn't mean I'll allow it to distract me.

"While I appreciate this wasn't your decision to make, I need you to listen carefully now. I am not in need of a guard, nor am I a child in need of babysitting. So, I release you."

She arches one perfect eyebrow, and a glint of a smile etches on her lips. It looks good on her. Too good. I step away, shaking my head from the odd hypnotism. Is that an immortal power? Are they meant to ensnare us, like we ensnare humans?

"What did you say?"

"I said, oh mighty Hades, that while that is all nice and good, you cannot release me."

"Why not?"

May the gods help me with this one. "Are you master of this realm?"

I scowl. "No."

"Then, you cannot undo this. Only the master of the realm can. Which, if I'm not mistaken, is Zeus."

A near-growl slips through my gritted teeth. "You know full well it's Zeus."

"I was humoring you." *And trying to get you off the topic before you do something stupid.*

Much as I want to dignify the latter with a response, I scoff in anger and move away from the door. Might as well concede I've lost control—for now.

Pegasus strides in a few hours later, his eyes wild until they settle on me. He clasps his chest like I've just saved him from dying.

"That's not nice, leaving me alone without even a note!" *And with Fenrir on the loose.*

I jerk my head toward Ileana. "Wasn't my decision."

Pegasus takes her in, unbearably slow. *Mm, I can understand how she'd make him follow. Hell, for a taste of that, I'd do anything.*

I clear my throat. Last thing I need is my best friend's salacious thoughts in my head.

"It's not like you to keep them after the fact," Pegasus drawls as he sits in a chair opposite me. "Dear, grab us some ambrosia, would you?"

I open my mouth to correct him, but Ileana is already moving. Or, rather, making things move. With one flick of her wrist, an entire decanter of ambrosia floats to us — without glasses. I realize a moment too late her intent when the entire content explodes in our faces.

Spluttering and wiping myself, I scowl at her. "Was that necessary?"

No. But it was satisfying. She only smiles coolly, and I have to admire she's holding her own against an Olympian, yet again.

The attitude she hides under all that light reminds me of the woman earlier. The one from the party, who'd distracted me. With everything else going on, I should have forgotten her. So why am I thinking of her now, when I'm faced with her exact opposite?

Pegasus stares between us, then gets up and finds some linen to wipe the mess. Since it's useless with me, I pull off my shirt and exchange it for another. No snarky remarks. Hmm. When I glance at Ileana over my shoulder, she's looking anywhere but at me.

Doubly intriguing. Perhaps she's not as immune to my charms as she'd like to pretend.

I toss another shirt to Pegasus, and he takes his time getting changed.

"Zeus seems to think I need a guard," I try to explain. "He's assigned this one to me. Her name's Ileana."

"Lower deity?"

"Immortal."

Pegasus' eyes widen. I should have paid more attention when he was talking about them, but now I can't pry more information out of him. Not with *her* here.

"I know you're a busy man, so we can catch up later." As I move him to the door, I whisper in his ear, "I need you to find out everything you can about immortals. I'll figure out a way to get it from you without Ileana knowing."

"You don't trust her?"

"Not yet."

After Pegasus leaves, I roam mindlessly in my room. This would be the time I'd drink myself into oblivion and not care what anyone thinks of me. And... Why the hell not?

Just because Zeus decided to further restrict my freedom with a babysitter doesn't mean I'm going to change. I've already conformed enough to last me an entire lifetime—and not the regular human length.

I stop my pacing and grab another

decanter of ambrosia, pouring some in a goblet. I hold it to Ileana, but she shakes her head. With a shrug, I swallow the whole thing, then pour myself another.

Wonderful. A drunkard, too. Only thing missing is him trying to seduce me.

Out of the corner of my eye, I take her in again. She has a radiance about her, a femininity that's unlike what I would expect from a protector. How is this tiny thing supposed to save my life, if it comes to it?

I swallow more ambrosia and force myself to face her. "When did Zeus ask you? To become my guard."

She shrugs. "Does it matter?"

"To me, it does."

How peculiar this one is. Out loud, she says, "The request came through a few days ago."

So, it had nothing to do with Fenrir. Interesting. Even more so is the fact Zeus must have asked her *before* my latest outburst.

"Waste of time, if you ask me," I say.

"You would say that to get rid of me, no?"

I want to glare at her, but the brilliance of her gaze makes it hard to hold it long enough.

I turn away, refusing to feel inferior yet again. I've had enough of that. Enough of Olympus. Enough of my brother. Enough of prisons.

"I need a walk."

Ileana follows me, of course. It's not until I'm on my way to the well-manicured gardens that I remember the nymph, and my brother, and everything that supposedly happens in this little labyrinth.

The plan isn't fully thought of. I figure, since she's already averse to me, maybe if I push her buttons the only way I know, it will get her to back off. Request a transfer. Or something. Whatever way this all works. Patience isn't my forte, and who knows when I'll see Pegasus again to get the information I need?

"So, did you go to school for, ah, guardianship?"

"You could say that."

I throw her a look. "You could give me more information, you know. Who would I tell?"

She huffs out a breath. "Fine. Yes, I went to school for this."

"Where, exactly?"

"In the midst of the Carpathians." *In a location unknown to mortals and gods alike, and it shall remain so.*

I can't deny the curiosity poking me. "And, what? You're taught how to fight?"

"In a way, yes. There are rigorous training exercises we must learn, if we are to protect a specific someone. And with gods, there is no room for error."

"I see. What happens if there is an error?"

I die. She clears her throat. "Not a good outcome."

"I heard we had zmei for protection, a while back."

She makes a sound of disgust. "Mindless creatures, ruled by impulse. They can be good in a fight because of their elemental powers and monstrous appearance, but useless otherwise."

"Hmm. I found them quite useful." A lie. I've never seen one in my existence, and the first I heard of them was through Pegasus. But I want to see if she'll take the bait.

Whether Ileana sees through my bullshit or not, she says nothing. Our walk brings us to the path, the area I'd been waiting for. Narcissus flowers are in full bloom, the air is filled with a heady fragrance, and water runs in sparkling rivers everywhere we turn. It's a little slice of heaven, one of my own creation.

"This is beautiful." Though she tries to keep the awe out of her voice, it's there.

Anyone would be impressed with Olympus, to be fair. Many pantheons have tried to outdo us, but none have quite managed it. Of course, my brother's crazy ideas of modernization will soon ruin the last of the peace we have here, but that's beside the point.

I pivot to her, stepping closer. "I could try for something as cliché as 'so are you' but somehow I doubt that will make an impact."

Ileana only stares back, ever the composed one. "Impact on what?"

Let's see if I can melt some of that iciness.

I take one more step, bringing us within touching distance. At the same time, I toss my goblet to the side and wrap an arm around her waist, pulling her closer against me. Her breathing comes to a full stop, and she stares at me, her sun-filled eyes wide and unreadable. But her lips part—whether to yell at me, or ask for a kiss, I don't wait to find out.

Instead, I go for a taste of her lips, teasing them with light strokes. Her mouth opens to me, and I don't hesitate to go in for the kill. Only, the joke's on me. Because the more I kiss her, the more I find her cinnamon taste appealing, and like the way her body fits mine.

This is bad. So bad. So, so bad.

I don't know where her thoughts stop and mine begin. There's too much to distract me, too much to…

Then something zaps me away, and I land a few feet farther. I stare at Ileana, thinking it had been her, but she's as shocked as I am. And then her training slams in, and she whirls on whoever attacked me, her hands lit with magic.

It's my first time experiencing *why*, exactly, immortals make great guards. And the quickness of Ileana's movements, the power I sense emanating from her hands, plus the barrier she has erected around me, are definitely points in her favor. They also distract me from our attacker, at least at first.

The man there is blond, with blue eyes. His loose black pants and white shirt ensemble is completed by a sword, slung by his hip. His cool gaze assesses me, but the smirk on his lips is all for Ileana. "Did I interrupt something, *partneră*?"

"Partner?" I ask, automatically translating from the dialect he uses.

Ah nu, nu, nu! Anyone but him. Ileana's distress doesn't come through to her expression, but I cannot ignore it. Not after that kiss.

I stand, dusting myself and nearing them both. "So, I'm gifted with not one, but two of you?"

The man mock bows toward me. "Făt-Frumos, at your service."

I shake my head. "What is it with your names?"

He shrugs. "You may call me Frumos, if the full name itself is too...complicated."

"Uh-huh." I ignore the jab and focus on Ileana. Instead of shying away from my gaze, she meets it fully. It's weird to talk about that in front of an audience but... "About the kiss."

"Momentary insanity," she says quickly. "Will not happen again."

"Damn well, it will not," Frumos adds. "We are here to protect him, not get in bed with him."

I scowl at him, unable to hold back the taunt. "You're not my type."

"Neither are you, oh mighty Hades."

It's my turn to arch an eyebrow. "Do they teach you that in school?"

Frumos glances at Ileana. "Been sharing some secrets?"

I may murder him before this assignment is done. Out loud, she says, "Nu. Only what is public knowledge."

"Right." He inspects the surroundings, his thoughts oddly protected. Either that, or he doesn't have much of them. "Where do we sleep, then?"

With a sigh, I head back to my quarters. I'd been hoping for nothing more than a night of oblivion. Only, that's to be denied to me, given both of my guards will now shadow my every step. How the hell am I supposed to keep my thoughts to myself? And ignore theirs?

We're nearing my chambers when I run into none other than Zeus.

"Brother dear," I drawl. "Care to explain my new babysitters?"

He faces me, ignoring said guardians. "For your protection. I've assigned a few all around."

It takes all my willpower not to punch him. Surely doing so in front of my guards, and anyone else who might notice, will only enlist more people against me. Contrary to belief, Olympians do love him.

"Why?" I settle for asking.

"Preventative measures."

"For?"

Zeus sighs. "Must you question everything? Take my word for it." *For once, just once, be like all of us and listen to this small thing. Then I won't have to think of ways to cover your ass when you screw up again. To hide that which sets you apart, makes you so abnormal... Which could be the end of me as a ruler. All because you can't be bothered to conform.*

I ignore his thoughts—they've been on repeat for the better part of the last millennia. Instead, I head to my door, pushing past him.

He grunts and moves backward, allowing me this small victory. As I open the door, though, I recall my promise to Pegasus. And unlike most Olympians, I stand by my promises.

Biting back a sigh, I turn to him. "All these measures… They wouldn't have anything to do with a certain Norse dog attacking me, would they?"

Zeus blanches. "When did that happen?"

"I would have thought Hermes told you."

"He did not. Are you all right?"

I shrug off his hand. "Fine. Don't pretend you care."

His eyes grow cooler, and he stands straighter. "Very well. Then I trust you'll have no issues with your new guards."

"I have issues, and plenty," I mutter. "But we'll survive."

He leaves, and I have no further answers than I did before. Biting back a curse, I open the doors to my rooms and wave Ileana and Frumos in. "All yours."

I head for the decanter of ambrosia, trying to ignore their thoughts and whispered conversation. Clearly, they know each other. And clearly, there's no way out of this. What did Zeus do, to provoke the Norse gods? Or, more in particular, Fenrir? He must've, since I was the one attacked. That part, I'm sure of. But what the hell does it all mean?

That night, once I pass out from the drink, I dream of the wolf... And then of a female laugh, locks of dark hair, and a scent that's definitely not cinnamon.

CHAPTER FOUR

Does he ever get out of bed?

A myriad of confusing thoughts bursts through my subconscious, rightfully waking me up. Ileana's by my window, glaring outside.

And why, out of all the people in the realms, did it have to be Făt who joins me on this assignment?

Ah, they do have a history. I wonder, based on his reaction yesterday, what it might be. Could be fun playing with my new guards, at least for the time being. If nothing else, it would distract from their annoying thoughts, their constant presence, and the fact I've been officially deemed incapable of taking care of myself.

I stretch in bed, and the movement draws Ileana's attention. The silky sheets drop to my waist, and she spends a moment longer staring, then turns away.

Between Făt and this cocky god, I will lose my mind. Or I may just murder one of them.

That, or end up in my bed. Perhaps. I don't want to encroach on another man's territory, and Frumos seems fairly possessive. But it would be extremely fun, especially given Ileana's prickliness.

Smirking, I get up and move to the bathtub. Similarly to Hera, I rather enjoy a hot bath every once in a while. Especially with a drink or two. A wave of my hand has the tub filling with steamy water. A moment later, I sink in with a satisfied sigh, holding a new cup of ambrosia.

Must he drink all the time?

"You can save your judgement." I only realize my mistake once heavy silence follows my words.

"I said nothing," Ileana murmurs.

Fuck. Day two of this, and I've already

messed up. How much longer until they both figure out my secret?

I doubt Zeus' intent in getting me two guards was to have me blurt out all my dirty deeds. But how could he not have grasped the dangers involved? At least if I sulk and hide in my chambers most of the time, I'm not seen. Gods and goddesses aren't around me long enough to understand there's something actually wrong with me. They just assume I don't fit into their little team.

Which, I don't.

Harsh ruminations for early morning… Much as I try to snap out of them, the usual wave of despair has already hit me. My limbs grow heavy and my eyes droop with fatigue. I take a deep swallow of ambrosia and stare at the foamy water. Imagining what it would be like, just once, to have full silence in my head. *Perhaps if the water covers me…*

Ileana moves into my line of sight, her eyebrows drawn together. "How did you know what I was thinking?"

"Don't be ridiculous, of course I didn't." I take a sip of the nectar and sink farther in. The bubbles protect most of my nudity, not that I'm purposefully hiding myself. "The judgment is plain as day on your face, is all."

"You had your back to me."

"I saw it when waking up." Taking another gulp, I keep my gaze on hers. "You know, there are better ways of waking up than that."

She scoffs, the tension leaving her expression. "You wish."

"Mm."

Ileana rolls her eyes and moves away from me, and I let the water restore my senses. My words may have put her off the scent, but I'll have to be careful. Zeus is already on my case, and he won't like it if anyone else knows of my...abilities. To be frank, I'm not quite sure he'd let them live to spread the tale. At the end of the day, it's not like any other gods have manifested with similar deficiencies. Which makes me special, but not in the best of ways.

Between the nectar, Ileana's silence—including her thoughts, oddly—and the hot water, I soon drift to sleep. But instead of the quietude of my dreams, I'm assailed by a nightmare.

I'm in a crowd, thoughts being thrown at me right and left. No matter how I try to ignore them, to make my way past them, the deities close in on me, surrounding me. Their judging eyes, their hardened stares, their thoughts permeate my mind until they're all I hear.

And then, when I think I can't take any more, someone laughs. The crowd parts. And a woman steps between them. At first, I think the deities are being deferential to her. It's only as she approaches that I notice they're turning their backs on her. Tears bathe her face, but her features are blurry. All I can see are her raven locks, a curvaceous body, and...a glowing gaze that traps me in its depths.

Hades...

I jerk up, splashing water everywhere. Somewhere behind me, Ileana snorts, but my mind is not on her. Not anymore. That woman...that voice... Why is she so familiar? And why did that nightmare leave me with such a sense of wrongness?

"Harsh wake-up?" Ileana says.

She keeps herself out of my sight. No way

I'm giving in to that trap. So instead of answering, I stand from the water, naked, and turn to her. Making sure I see her mouth if she speaks, rather than answer her thoughts. This one's too perceptive right now.

Since I can't know whether what she asked me was spoken out loud or not, I retort with another question. "Where's your partner?"

"Out."

"Does he do that often?"

"How would I know? This is our first assignment." She averts her stare from me. "And would it kill you to put on some clothes?"

I laugh. "You know us Olympians, we love flaunting what we have." With unbearably slow movements, I place my goblet on a small table and rifle through some clothes before donning a shirt and loose pants. Then I turn to Ileana. "Better?"

She refuses to dignify that with an answer.

Well, well. It won't stop me from baiting her some more. "As for your partner... Could have fooled me. Thought I detected some history."

The only history comes from his idiotic self thinking he is superior to me.

I don't fall for it this time, instead waiting. Out loud, all Ileana says is, "No history." *Interesting.*

Sometimes, despite hearing thoughts, I like to pretend I'm not quite there. People talk a lot around someone when they think he's either sleeping or unaware. And the immortals are no exception, as I come to realize when Frumos returns.

His energy is unique, enough that I feel him nearing before he's actually here. Since I haven't said a word to Ileana in the last half an hour, it's easy to let my head loll to the side of the couch and pretend to be asleep.

The moment the door opens, Ileana is on him, her voice low and annoyed. "Where the hell have you been?"

"Around."

"Not good enough. We are to be partners in this, you cannot just go off on your own."

"Partners? Do not make me laugh, *draga mea.* You were already entangled with the god the minute I walked in. I think you already found your partner."

There's the sound of a scuffle, enough to intrigue me, and I crack an eye open. Ileana must've tried to slap him, because he has her hand in a tight vise-like grip, and they're both busy glaring at each other.

Tension indeed. History, too.

I close my eyes again. Ileana's panting and annoyed grunt makes me think she probably tried to slap him with her other hand.

"Hand fighting is not your forte, we both know it," Frumos says.

"Just because you bested me once—"

"More than once, and there were witnesses. Let it go, Ileana."

A huff of displeasure from her, followed by a chuckle from him. It soon dies off at her next words.

"If I did not know better, I would assume you are jealous."

There's a long silence, almost long enough peek my interest. But I don't chance it. Instead, I focus on his thoughts, actively seeking them out as he speaks.

"Jealous? Of a Greek god? Please." *The only thing I am jealous of is that he gets to put his hands on you, when you deny me over and over. Two hundred years is a long time to go reminiscing of that one night together, beautiful Ileana. But the best is yet to come.*

He clears his throat. "Now, enough with the foolishness. Will you listen to what I have to say?" Silence for a beat, and I sense his eyes on me. "Is he truly asleep?"

"Ambrosia first thing in the morning will do that to a person, god or not. What is it?"

Frumos doesn't mince words. "Despite what you might have been thinking, I was not out frolicking or wasting time. Zeus requested my presence this morning, before you were awake."

"Why you? Why not us both?"

"My guess? You being a woman plays a part in it."

"I swear, Făt, I *will* hit you this time—"

"Breathe. *I* do not mean it that way. Only that *he* probably has enough emotional females around him." Another chuckle. "Hera was yelling at him when I walked in."

"So the rumors are true?"

"Of his infidelity? Clearly. Besides, count yourself lucky. Better to stay out of his way, lest his lecherous gaze lands on you."

The thought of my brother wanting anything to do with Ileana is enough to get my blood boiling, but I force myself to remain unaffected. It won't do for them to realize I can, in fact, hear them, and I'm wide awake.

"Point taken. But I would appreciate being included in further conversations."

"As you wish. Now, can I get to the meat of the problem?" Ileana must assent in some way, because Frumos continues. "We were not told everything, when we took this on. Either that, or things have developed, and rapidly."

"Very well… Color me intrigued. How so?"

"What were you told about this assignment, exactly? I know you were spoken with at a separate time than me and sent here earlier. Probably in a way to make the transition easier, given you are female. But I am curious about the specifics of what you were told."

I'm also more curious than I'd like to admit. How much *did* Zeus reveal, or did he reveal anything at all? I would expect he hadn't. Since I'm so special, and so threatening—at least according to my brother—it would make more sense to keep me under wraps. But then what the hell is Frumos going on about, implying there's more to this than simply protecting me?

"My trainer only said that Zeus' brother keeps getting into trouble and needs someone to keep an eye on him."

So it wasn't Zeus himself who sought them, but he went through an intermediary?

"Same as me, then."

Exasperation coats Ileana's voice. "Get to the point, Făt. And sometime this century, please."

I find it even more intriguing he asks everyone else to call him Frumos, yet she calls him Făt. A question for another day…

"Impatient, are we? Ow! All right, no need to hit me. And you wonder why you were not involved— *All right*, do not start with the foolishness again. I will tell you. Zeus revealed Hades was attacked by a Norse wolf yesterday."

"Yes, I was already aware. And I did tell you last night, only you were not listening."

"I do not recall it."

Neither do I. Was I so gone, their talk didn't even wake me? Weird. Not to mention their formal way of speaking is starting to jar my nerves.

Ileana continues, "Besides, it is not that surprising, given the pantheons all cohabitate, to some extent. Bored minds lead to drama, and the deities are prone to it."

It's funny—sometimes—to hear how others talk about us. We don't cohabitate, per se. That would imply we're all in the same realm. Rather, the reality is each pantheon has its own realm, responsible for one area of the world, with an atrium for Council business.

"Perhaps," Frumos says. "But this was no simple wolf. Do you remember Fenrir?"

"Yes... We both met him. He has no angry bone in his body."

"I could disagree with that. There is a reason the Norse gods imprisoned him, and did you forget he bit someone's arm off?"

"Exaggerations."

She sounds more and more like me. Perhaps we've both been raised to give a second chance to the underdogs…

The silence that follows intrigues me. I open my eyes again, watching for a moment as they face off against each other. Then I close them again.

"Sure. So how then do you explain him going after one of Olympus' princes?" Frumos asks.

"I cannot."

"That is where you are wrong, Ileana. Something—"

And as is my luck, Pegasus chooses that moment to burst through the door. To keep up the ruse, I pretend to snap awake, rubbing at my eyes.

"Hades, you have to come. Now." *Before shit gets fucked.*

Something in his tone tells me whatever it is, it's bad. Combined with what I heard from the immortals, none of it bodes well. And for once, it trumps my need for entertainment.

I follow Pegasus out the door, my new shadows behind us. When he takes me away from the main areas and toward the gardens, the feeling in my gut intensifies enough to physically make me sick.

Pray to Orion and back he doesn't lose it. Pegasus' internal monologue doesn't help.

I push on until we get there, but I'm starting to guess what we're about to find.

The garden is destroyed. *My* garden. Like some troll has trampled all over it.

Instead of the gorgeous narcissus, the roses, and other human flowers I'd replicated, there is nothing left standing. *Nothing.* Only shattered leaves and petals coat the ground. The earth itself looks like it was raked by claws.

"Am I missing something?" Frumos asks. "These are only flowers, and no cause for mourning."

In my anger, I turn on him. My punch meets his jaw, but the second gets stopped by his fist.

Eyes narrowed, he warns, "I am here to protect you, not fight you."

"Too bad."

I yank my wrist out of his grip and elbow him in the gut. He bends over, and I vaguely hear Ileana calling out—but I'm too far gone. Blind rage fills me. Why must everything here end in disaster? Why must everything of *mine* be seen as less than, a perfect target for those in need of distractions?

I punch Frumos again, getting ready to kick him next. Then Pegasus steps between us, separating us.

"Enough, Hades," he whispers as he holds me back. "I know you're hurting, but enough."

I snap to, taking in everything once more. The destruction. The bewildered gazes. Then I shrug off Pegasus' hold and march off.

I'm not alone, at least not for long. Ileana follows me and shoves me into the closest wall. It reverberates when my body strikes it, once more making me aware of her power.

Ileana's expression is easily as angry as mine. "You being a god does not give you the rights you seem to be taking. First with kissing me, then treating Făt as your punching bag. Deal with your issues, Hades, but leave us out of it."

Watching as she storms away, it hits me for the first time that maybe, just maybe, I lashed out at the wrong people.

When I enter my quarters much later, it's to find Ileana and Frumos deep in conversation.

"I owe you both an apology," I mutter. "That garden wasn't just a patch of earth with flowers. Our mother, Rhea, taught us from a young age how to nurture our powers. Not all gods and goddesses are alike, though. And there are some who simply don't come into their powers right away, or don't know how to use them. I was helping the young ones, and that garden was our safe space." Before all of Olympus started shunning me, that is. I take a deep breath. "Whoever did this must have known of it. Must have known it would affect me, and more than me. We need to tell Zeus."

"We already have," Ileana says. "And he has requested you do not leave the immediate area for the time being."

"Of course he did."

She shares a look with Frumos, then arches an eyebrow my way.

With a sigh, I turn to him. "I am sorry, for lashing out at you."

He inclines his head ever so, but it's not quite a forgiveness. Whoever knew immortals could be prouder than gods?

"And for what it's worth, I am also sorry for kissing you," I tell Ileana. Is that surprise or hurt in her expression? Whatever it is, it's gone too soon for me to make up my mind, and her thoughts give me no clue.

"You are not here for my personal enjoyment but to protect me," I continue. "I will respect that, going forward, in as much as I possibly can."

Which, one hopes, will be enough to keep me in line.

Talk about an apology, Frumos scoffs internally.

Ileana's thoughts are still oddly silent, but she glances at him. Some kind of unspoken communication goes between them.

"What's the look for?" I ask. "Do you both know something I should?"

"We do," Frumos says. "Zeus called me in this morning to warn about Fenrir and his attack on you. Something has stirred the Norse gods into a frenzy, and they are getting unruly. Zeus does not know why, but a Council meeting will take place soon to determine what the issue is, and attempt to mediate it."

"Am I permitted to attend?"

Frumos shrugs. "To my knowledge, Zeus did not say otherwise, so I would assume yes."

"When is it?"

"Tonight."

"Good. Then you will both accompany me." I move to the decanter of ambrosia, considering the conversation closed.

"Is that really the best idea?" Ileana asks, gesturing to the liquid.

"It keeps me hydrated," I shoot back. "And calm. So, yes, it is."

You don't want to know me without it, believe me. Not when everyone and their nymphs' thoughts get at me, breaking at my consciousness. Gods are trained in using their magic, the powers they are innately born with, of course. But as for their minds? It's a given they'll be perfect, much like their outside shell. Evidently, that particular rule skipped me, otherwise there would be a cure for my affliction.

Which, there is not, as I concluded after

eons of searching for it.

Another strong gulp later, I turn to them. "Did Zeus happen to mention what got them in a frenzy?"

"He did not," Ileana says. "But he seemed scared."

I snort into my cup. "My brother doesn't get scared."

Even as I say it, I doubt it. The other night, when I'd mentioned Fenrir, there had been a definite expression of fear on his face. What could it mean, though? What will it lead to, even? The pantheons have coexisted peacefully for ages. To think of discord...

My gut twists, an unwelcome feeling of foreboding. I wash it away with more ambrosia.

CHAPTER FIVE

I dream once more of long, raven hair and a scent that stirs my senses. I can't make out her features, no matter how hard I try, but that laugh… I want to bottle it up and keep it for darker days.

I can't remember the last time I had such elusive dreams, and it's both infuriating and intriguing. Even in a half-awake state, I promise myself to head back to the human realm, and see if I can find her again. Whoever she is. Surely she can't be a figment of my imagination only?

"Hades! *Hades!*"

The hiss of a low voice wakes me up, and I

groan, wiping a hand over my face. I blink a few times, and become aware of an unnatural stillness in the room. A glance to my door shows Ileana and Frumos, standing straight as arrows and awaiting orders. Past them is a nymph, her translucent form as alluring as she is annoyed.

Why they had to send me to get this one...

When my gaze settles on her, she flushes and bows. "Lord Hades, your presence is requested in the atrium."

"By whom?" My voice is hoarse.

"Zeus, my lord."

I nod and wave her away, then face my guards. "Looks like the Council met sooner rather than later." Odd. Normally it takes them days to convene, not mere hours.

"What makes you say that?" Frumos asks.

"Zeus would not have sent a nymph to get me otherwise."

I turn my back on them and shed my clothes, then step into the bathtub. Someone clears their throat.

"Shouldn't you hurry?"

"I'm not important enough to hold them back. Believe me, we won't miss anything crucial."

Except perhaps the reason for this whole debacle.

I choose to ignore Ileana's thought, instead focusing on washing the scent of ambrosia off me.

By the time I step through the massive doors of the atrium, Ileana and Frumos on my heels, it is packed to the brink. There must be more than sixty, seventy Olympians here, and not just the more reputable gods. I can see Hephaistos, Bacchus, and others in corners, whispering and frowning. Annoyingly enough, I'm not the only one with guards, and I wonder what, exactly, is going on.

My gaze roams the area. Large, dark marble columns create a circle in the middle and support a golden dome. A floating torch hangs from each column, sending flickers of flames through the room and illuminating it. Each column has a chair in front of it, occupied by one of the pantheons' representatives.

Zeus is on his throne in the middle,

facing a few others from various pantheons. There's Amun with the Egyptians, his kohl-rimmed eyes narrowed. He's head of Egyptian pantheon, much like Zeus plans to be for Olympus.

Then there's Odin, with the Norse, his worn features drawn more than usual, a patch over his bad eye. Out of all of us, the Norse are the only ones who don't hide their so-called human flaws. Well, that's not entirely true. They hide plenty—which is why I avoid their thoughts like the plague.

My gaze continues surveying everyone, landing on Morrigan. I'd recognize that Celtic face in a million after our last encounter. She winks at me, then focuses her attention back on the proceedings.

If there's ever been a truer queen, I've yet to meet her. Morrigan is as close to perfection as I've ever come, and unlike the rest of the pantheons who stay away from me on account of Zeus' machinations, she's only ever been a friend. A great friend, at that. Despite the fact she's part of her own trinity that rules over the Celts, and thus is bound by other loyalties, her status as a sorceress has garnered her some...freedoms. More than me, that's for sure.

That's a lot of deities, Ileana thinks. I make an effort not to reply, at least until she asks out loud. "Are there always this many of them?"

"No. They usually come alone, not with entourages."

And there are *many.* Too many. Much more than I would have expected for some disturbed gardens and a wolf god missing...

Another voice says, "The last time we all met was when we decided to retire."

I turn to Pegasus, grasping his forearm in our usual greeting and lowering my voice. "What is all this?"

He shrugs, though it's not his usual careless one. "Not sure, brother. Let us hear it out."

We all face the gods. Zeus nods my way—in a silent warning to behave—then pivots to everyone else once more. It seems we really didn't miss much, other than introductions.

"Odin, before we begin proceedings, I would need you—or one from your pantheon—to explain why my brother was attacked by Fenrir the demon hound."

Odin's taped-off eye seems to twitch, and his clear eye flashes with indignation. "What proof do you have?"

Without wanting to, I get dragged into his thoughts. Though he thinks in some Nordic dialect, I have been around long enough to understand.

If he cannot prove it, none of the other gods will rebel against us. I will not risk what I know, not when the danger itself could be lying in wait here.

What the hell is the old fool going on about? I clench my fist, wanting to intervene. As brother to Zeus, I could. But it seems I do not have to.

"Proof?" Zeus rumbles, standing. "My brother was chased down on some earthly realm."

Hmm. I wouldn't have expected him to be so…protective. Especially of me. Unless this is a show designed to make sure his reputation blossoms. As a perfect leader…the best one Olympus could have.

"That cannot be," Odin says. "Fenrir would not enter Midgard."

Right. Or attack a god. Or bite another god's hand. Because gods never do anything remotely flawed. Ever. The vehemence of Frumos' thoughts surprises me, but I don't acknowledge them.

"Perhaps there is another explanation," Morrigan adds, ever the pacifist. "Could we speak to Fenrir?"

"No." Odin clears his throat, as if realizing he spoke too abruptly. "He is unavailable for an audience."

"Convenient," Zeus throws.

Despite his bravado, his thoughts betray his uneasiness. *This is the second incident, we need to get to the bottom of it.*

Second incident? What the hell was the first?

I glance at Pegasus, but of course he's unaware of my brother's thoughts. No one else heard, except for me. And once more, in a sea of people, I'm all alone.

"What are you accusing us of, exactly?" Odin's son, Thor, stands to his feet and inches closer.

Him and Zeus could be brothers, though he is taller and broader in shoulders. He could probably squash Zeus, if he didn't get zapped first. I smile at the thought, but not for long.

As their voices rise, the cacophony of their thoughts also increases. The crescendo is something I cannot avoid, rising to the point it engulfs everything else in my mind. The audience hall fades away, and only the voices are left.

This is getting out of control—

Why must Thor always cause trouble?

As always, the Norse and Olympians at each other's throats—

Someone deescalate this before they get to blows and embarrass us al!

Then my brother makes it worse. "Hades, come up front." When I don't move, rooted to the spot by my attempts to ignore the noise, he asks, louder, "Hades!"

Ileana pushes me forward, following in my footsteps. Only, I stumble, and the voices grow even louder.

Drunk again.

Disgrace to his brother.

Who's to say his story is the truth, not a demand for more attention?

Disgrace. Disgrace. Disgrace.

I bow my head, holding on to the side with my free hand, groaning. I catch Ileana's glance. She must realize something's wrong with me, as she steps closer. Her presence is a nice comfort, but then her own thoughts turn to our kiss, and that makes it worse.

"Hades, testify what you have seen."

I try, blindly, to focus on my brother. Somehow, I make it into the circle. The flickering torches set the rest of audience to shadows, but their thoughts are ever more present, to the point I cannot hear my own.

Liar.

Disgrace.

Embarrassment to Zeus.

"I..."

Zeus glares at me, then takes a step closer, hissing, "Pull yourself together!"

I straighten my back at the admonishment, and clear my throat. A dull throb has started on one side of my head, but I ignore it, trying to focus on speaking.

"Fenrir attacked me in darkness, near a human village party. Hermes helped send him off, otherwise he could have harmed me. I've no idea why he did so."

Only, what comes out of my mouth is not the dialect I'd meant. Instead of the soft vowels of human dialect, which we've adopted, the words are rough growls, guttural sounds. The language of the Titans. The one banned from Olympus around the same time as our father.

Zeus stares at me in shock—then the uproar explodes.

Gods freaking out over my use of the Old Tongue. Goddesses swarming to the Council, demanding answers. And through it all, I'm aware of my brother's glare, and Odin's. And the confused expressions of the other gods.

"Enough!" I roar, clutching my head and bending at the waist.

Ileana is there, and Frumos, surprisingly. They hoist me by the elbows and pull me away, Ileana leading the charge.

"We need to get him out!" she whispers to him, and somehow her words carry across.

Somewhere between leaving and the cacophony, I pass out.

It wouldn't be the first time all the mental strain has led me to hallucinate. But, more often than not, I regain consciousness and land in pleasant dreams. This time, when I next wake up, it's to their faint arguing.

"You must have picked up on it, too!"

"I do not know what you mean."

"Ileana, enough. You are far too smart to fall for a god's charming body. Do not take me for a fool."

A bark of laughter escapes me, and I mutter, "Thanks for the compliment, immortal. Should I be concerned your affections sway toward me?"

"Do not flatter yourself," Frumos says as he comes closer. His eyes are narrowed on my slouched, albeit limp, form. "You looked better before."

"I've felt better." I rub the back of my neck and try to stand, almost succeeding. "What happened?"

"We were hoping you could tell us," Ileana says. Her eyes won't leave me, as if she's expecting me to shatter. "Since when do you speak the Old Tongue?"

It's my turn to frown. "Since when do *you*

know the Old Tongue?"

They share a glance, and Frumos says, "We were taught it in school. In order to protect all deities, we must be well-versed in everything. Including things of old. Including…the forbidden. And we must rise above it."

"Hmm. Doesn't that get tiring?"

Frumos rolls his eyes. "Yes, but we were created for such a purpose. If you think we are straight arrows, you should have seen the other dozen immortals in our school. Each more perfect than the last." *And yet it was I who Ileana chose that night…* He shakes his head, as if to remove the thought. "We cannot complain, we each have our purpose."

"So you, what, simply accept this path laid out for you?"

"It is our only path," he says. "It is what we were created for, our entire race. To protect the gods. Forever." He glances at Ileana and some of his cool expression falters for a moment, then the mask is back on. "Not all of us may agree with it, but unless we are dismissed from our role, we have no choice. It simply…is."

"I see." I'm reminded of Ileana refusing my dismissal, saying only Zeus could do it since he's master of this realm. What a damn mess. Maybe I'm not the only one stuck in a life I hate, after all.

Ileana clears her throat. "So, the Old Tongue? I thought it was banned from Olympus, eons ago."

"It was," I mutter. "Because the Titans were set to sleep, and speaking their language, some would say, could raise them again."

"Not something you would want," Frumos says. "They were your biggest threat, once upon a time. If the pantheons had not worked together, you probably would have all been extinguished."

"I see you are most definitely versed in our history." They both ignore my bitterness. "Anyway, point of the matter is, Zeus, Poseidon, and I still speak it. But we're not supposed to."

"Then what made you speak it?" Ileana asks.

Frumos throws her a look, as if she should bite her tongue. Probably because she seems much too interested in me in this moment. I sigh, too tired to care for their little drama.

"I'm not sure. Must've been too drunk."

"See, I would believe that," Frumos says, "except you had no drinks before we left. What are you hiding, Hades?"

I push off the couch and move around. I shouldn't be making things worse, and this is specifically adding to it. How can I explain that I was so overwhelmed with everyone, and the words simply came? I reverted back to an old way of being, a way that is now banned. No pantheon will understand, nor will they forgive.

No. To everyone else's eyes, I am Hades, the black sheep of Olympus. The failure. The screw-up. The disgraced brother.

"Hiding?" I snort. "You assume I have enough brain cells left to come up with machinations after all my drinking. I assure you, I do not."

I walk away from them to a basin of water and splash some on my face. The throbbing in my head is not as deep, though it's still there. Odd, once more. Gods are not meant to experience physical distress. Yet another instruction my body seems to have missed out on.

After I wipe my face, I turn to my guards once more. "What happened after…?"

"Your odd seizure?" Ileana shrugs. "Last I heard was Zeus asking the Council for a break. Demanded Odin produce Fenrir to the next meeting."

"Wonderful." I eye the ambrosia decanter, but it's too far for me to envision grasping it. "And on a scale of one to enormous, how angry is my brother?"

"Very." The voice comes from the entrance. Zeus takes one look at my guardians and jerks his head to the outside.

Weirdly, I didn't even see him enter. Though I shouldn't be surprised, he was bound to come yell at me sooner rather than later.

As if to prove my point, once Ileana and Frumos are gone, he faces me and crosses his arms. "You couldn't well act the part, could you?" *All I needed was you to give me enough ammunition to bring the Norse down a few pegs. Then I could've found out what they're hiding.*

Somehow, the ambrosia doesn't seem so far away. I stumble to it and gulp a full goblet, then reach for another. Amid my noisy drinking, Zeus continues talking.

"I realize you and I are different, brother, but I had hoped to at least count on your assistance." *After all, you owe me.*

"Perhaps you could—if you bothered telling me what was going on."

Zeus' narrowed gaze stays on me, then flicks to the ambrosia. Smirking, I empty another goblet, then wipe my mouth and shrug. "Suit yourself."

"Wait." He sighs and gestures to the drink. "Pass me some."

Once I do, he paces, sipping it delicately.

"In my last earthly adventure—"

"You mean your frolicking."

"Yes, that." He sends an annoyed glance my way. "Something felt off. Like I was being followed. Two days later, Poseidon said some of his creatures turned against him." *I thought I only had your mind-reading to worry about, but it seems to be the least of my problems nowadays.*

I try to focus on the words he spoke out loud instead of the mess in his head. "What does that mean, exactly?"

Our brother lives in a realm under water.

He's always preferred it to being above ground, and says the world is much nicer and appealing. More than once, I've thought of escaping there, but he also doesn't want me around. Unsurprising.

"His creatures love him," I mutter.

"They do. He said something had taken control of them, possessed them, and they attacked him while he was out."

"That's not possible."

Zeus swallows heavily. "But it is. And it has happened again—with you. Only, this time, you were able to pinpoint a culprit."

Everything he's saying finally makes sense. Both of them attacked, now me... "You're saying someone's coming after us, because we're, what? Heirs?"

"Not just heirs," Zeus says. "But the rightful rulers of Olympus."

I barely hold back a snort. "Always playing politics, brother."

"At least I have a purpose." He winces, as though regretting his jab.

I let it go this time, instead focusing on his theory. "You think it's the Norse gods who were behind the other two incidents?"

"I do not want to believe it… But how else can we explain what happened?"

I shake my head, recalling Odin's wayward thoughts. "Would Odin know of it, then? It seems unlikely."

Zeus's expression hardens. "Whether he knows or not, it is his responsibility to fix it."

Yes, my brother and his black-and-white views. It's been so long since we've had conversations, that I've even forgotten how intrinsically annoying he can be.

"What if it's beyond him?"

He frowns at my question, and peers at me closer. "What do you know?"

"Nothing." And I don't, not really. Whatever I heard, I cannot say what it means. I most definitely can't pinpoint a culprit.

"I don't believe you." Zeus steps closer, an odd glint in his eyes. "You can help me in this, brother. Join the next meeting and tell me what's being thought."

"All of a sudden, I'm useful now?"

"For once, yes. Will you help me?"

I shake my head. Wanting to deny him. Knowing I can't. "Yes."

Satisfied, he leaves, and my guards step

back in the room shortly after. When I say nothing, simply stare out the window for an extended period, Ileana clears her throat.

"What was that about?"

"A way to make myself useful." I turn to them and force a grin. "I think another trip to Earth is needed."

"Not the best idea, given the circumstances," Frumos says.

"Perhaps. But I'm going regardless. One of you can come with me, or you can both stay here." I shrug. "Your choice."

If nothing else, I want to escape Olympus and the looks that will follow me around for the next few days. And... I want to find the woman. The one who's been showing up in my dreams, teasing me with her scent. I want to see if she's as interesting in person as my mind has made her out to be.

Before Ileana can say anything, Frumos steps forward. "I will come. Ileana can keep an eye on anything here that might be out of the ordinary."

Typical. Leave the female behind while they go have their male fun. And no, I do not care if part of that involves other females. What Făt and

I had was a long time ago, and it was a single night. Even if I cannot get it out of my head... Though her pinched expression says she's none too happy about being left behind, and her thoughts clearly imply there's more to it, she nods.

The moment after, Frumos opens a portal, and we go through it.

We emerge in a village similar to the previous one. No, not similar. It's the *same* village. I take in my surroundings, then face my immortal guard. "How did you know?"

He shrugs. "We are trained for this."

Trained to read my mind? I don't say the words out loud. Instead, I ask, "And why could we not come via the regular means?"

"If anyone is after you, it makes sense to vary your movements, no? An immortal's portal is more secure than a god materializing and dematerializing. Different magic, less traceable."

The logic of that is beyond anything I can comprehend, so I don't bother disputing it. "What makes you think anyone is after me?"

He smirks. "You just confirmed it."

Rolling my eyes, I step away from him and head closer to the sound of music and laughter. While the mortals' thoughts assail me, Frumos adds one more thing. "Are you planning to toy with Ileana's feelings?"

I toss him a glare over my shoulder. "It was not my intention."

"Then quit it." *She doesn't need your games*

How peculiar. His internal thoughts are very much focused on her, meaning he's far more connected to her than I gave him credit for.

"Far be it for me to step on another's territory."

He glowers at me. "She is not property."

"No... But she's clearly not meant to be mine, either."

Before he can say anything else, I lose myself in the crowd of humans. My habits already match theirs, and in their inebriated state they won't realize just how strange I am. Nor how I move differently than they do, more fluidly, more in tune with the energies that breathe life into them.

And if I don't find her...that woman... Then, soon enough, I may find some warm body to keep me company for the night, and make me forget.

Even as I think that, laughter grabs my attention. A particular laugh—one I've been hearing in my dreams. I stop dancing and turn, only to see a flash of raven hair.

CHAPTER SIX

Long, raven hair falls to her waist in thick, curly locks. She has on a simple dress, white with flowers on it. All that emanates from her is sunshine, laughter and…life.

How can a human hold this much joy? They're simple creatures, yes, not prone to the politics we play. Not prone to the weight of the world on their shoulders. Most of them live day by day, aware of their single purpose and tasking themselves with achieving it.

But this one…

Before I even know what I'm doing, I take a step toward her. Then another. This time, I don't hesitate. With assured strides, I make my way over.

She's dancing with a human, her lithe body swaying to the music. When she laughs, she throws her head back and laughs from her core. And still I'm drawn even closer, addicted to the sound, to hearing more of it. Who is this woman?

She whirls to the music, and then comes to an abrupt stop. Her eyes take me in, her entire being frozen. As am I.

She is beautiful, yes, but there's more to it than that. More than the rosebud mouth, the high cheekbones, the eyes that draw me in. The glint in them—that odd hue of violet—immediately tells me she is no human.

How could I have mistaken her for one, even from afar? The radiance surrounding her is enough to overshadow even Ileana's brilliance. Is she another immortal, meant to tease me into insanity?

Another step, and another, and finally I'm within an arm's reach.

Frumos is somewhere behind me, hovering, staring in confusion. *What's gotten into him?*

I can't explain his presence, nor can I take

my eyes off her. I'm not even drunk, yet I'm having a reaction like if I blink, she'll be gone, and I'll be left bereft. Of her presence, of her laugh, of…

While I stupidly attempt to get my thoughts back on track, she doesn't have that hesitation. One moment she's there, the next she's gone, only a flash of raven hair in the crowd.

"Oh no, you don't!"

I ignore Frumos' shouts and take off after her, catching up right as we reach the edge of the crowd. Without asking permission, I pull a Zeus and grab her hand, tugging her against me. I've never been one to cross personal boundaries without permission, but I can't allow her to leave. Not again.

"Going somewhere, beautiful?"

Her slap has me stumble and let her go. Surely, that's not how this goes for my brother when he approaches a woman… *Perhaps I'm simply rusty.* The stinging in my cheek tells me as much, and confirms she's also definitely not human. No human's slap could resonate this loud or hurt—*ow*—this much.

Frumos chooses that time to barge through

the crowd, hand on his sword. *Finally he gets his due.* His thought distracts me for a millisecond even as this mysterious goddess finally speaks.

"Just because you're a god of Olympus doesn't give you the right to manhandle everyone you come across."

My jaw is somewhere on the ground, but I pick it up and clear my throat. "How do you…?" I glance around, making sure no human can truly hear us. "How did you know?"

Frumos' eyes narrow. I wave for him to go away, but instead of listening, he spreads his feet apart and stares me down.

"Move," I order. "I have this under control."

"Yeah? Enough to realize she's also an Olympian, like you?"

I jerk toward her then. That radiance I'd seen, the eyes—

She cocks a hip and her violet gaze shoots bolts of lightning my way. "And if I am?"

"That's how you knew about me, then?"

She does scoff this time. "That, plus your swagger and bad attitude, for one."

"Funny. No humans complained before."

"Then how about you find one of them to keep you company?"

Clearly, I'm not making a very good first impression. "Are you saying if I tone it down, I'll have the pleasure of your company tonight?"

She makes a sound that might very well be a snort and taps her foot impatiently. Underneath the bravado, I sense something else. Not thoughts, per se, but again that oddity. Like I know her. But I don't. Except for my obsessive dreams, surely?

"I don't understand." I take a step closer. "How have I not seen you before?"

"Perhaps because on the rare instances I was there, you were drunk out of your mind."

Wow. It does not take much to get a god infatuated, I suppose. I ignore Frumos' thought, at first.

And then I realize the absence of something else. This woman, this goddess, whoever she is—I *cannot* hear her thoughts. It's not that there are none, that's impossible. But rather than all the gods whose thoughts attack me daily, hers are...not.

My entire focus becomes centered on her. My gaze slowly rakes her up and down, leaving me half-amused at the way she bristles under my inspection. And I listen with all my senses. Inhaling her sweet scent, feeling the sunshine emanating off her, but as far as her thoughts…there is nothing. Just her radiance and something else, underneath it all. Something…more. Something darker. The combination is too intriguing to pass up on, and I find myself wanting to stay with her longer.

"I would have remembered seeing you."

She crosses her arms. "May I leave, now? Or will you order me around, my lord?"

All right. If she wants me to act every bit the spoiled prince she thinks me to be, then it can be arranged. I straighten and level a hard gaze on her. "No, you may not. What is your name?"

My change of demeanor affects her, too. She drops the hand from her hip, and her attitude falters, if only for a second. She stares at me, lips parted, and something jolts again in my body. What blasted twist of the Fates is this?

I enter her personal space, and she tosses her head back to glare at me. I'd intended to catch her thoughts, but all I feel is that unnerving quiet.

"Your name." My voice comes out hoarse, more demanding this time.

She holds my gaze for another second, then looks away and mutters, "Persephone."

And then, when I'm unable to say or do anything else, she disappears into the crowd once more. I'm left staring after her, half wanting to chase her. But Zeus' brother doesn't chase after anyone, let alone an unknown goddess.

Persephone... Why do I know that name?

"Can we get back to Olympus now?"

I ignore Frumos, instead heading to the edge of the party. In the shadows, with Frumos watching over me, I observe Persephone. How she interacts with the humans, talks to them, laughs with them, completely free. I envy that freedom. I *want* that freedom. But it's as out of reach for me as she is.

By the time I finally tear my gaze from after her, the sun is already rising. I've spent the night watching her, and still, I have no more answers than I did before.

I turn to Frumos, and he's already opened

a portal. No human is around to notice, and he seems more than ready to head back home. I'm not, but I stumble after him anyway, drunk on more than ambrosia this time around.

The next day, as my guardians sleep, and no one else comes to visit, I spend it in a daze. Pacing and going out of my mind, repeating our conversation so many times, my head hurts.

Once I've done rehashing everything and beating myself over my first impression, I step onto the balcony and glare at the world. Night is almost here, and I have spent an entire day with my thoughts on this goddess.

Have my senses dulled so much that I'm out of touch with my deity powers? I should have felt Persephone's aura, should have known she was a goddess. An Olympian.

And yet I didn't. I'd thought she was a human, at best some kind of elfin creature or an immortal. But a goddess? The thought never hit me.

Granted, I've been out of touch with the Olympians. I've spent the last centuries more drunk than I have sober. Could it be she's a new goddess? It has been a while since we celebrated one's birth, which means that's probably not the case.

What am I missing?

And if I *am* missing things, it puts into question my meeting with Fenrir, too. What else did I miss, if I could miss out on a goddess' aura?

A darker thought rears its ugly head. What if Fenrir wasn't truly...himself? His thoughts spoke of *need*. Need what? Help? Blood? Restraint? It could've been all, or none. I never caught more, nor did I mention any of this to anyone else.

Sighing, I shift my gaze to the gardens below me. And something flashes in there, a silent appeal I'm all too familiar with. I turn and head back inside.

On my way out the door, I jostle Ileana awake. "Come with me. Someone's here to see me."

I could have left by myself, but I don't want them to get in trouble. It might have only been a few days, but I've come to realize I don't mind these guards all that much, at least not anymore. They're an acquired taste, but at the end of the day, they keep the loneliness at bay. And that, if nothing else, earns them my loyalty.

As we go out of the mansion, Ileana tries to stifle a yawn. "Are we meeting your mysterious new crush?"

I throw her an uneasy glance, only to see her smile.

"Do not fret, my lord. I jest."

I pause in my steps. My visitor won't wait forever, but I need to get this out. "About that kiss—"

Ileana holds a finger to my lips. "It was pleasant, but we both know our fates are not intertwined. At least, not in the way we would have thought originally."

I nod, having figured out much of the same myself.

"My question was innocent, I assure you."

"Ah. Then, no, it isn't my new crush, but perhaps this visitor can shed some light on what's going on."

We continue walking, and then we emerge

into the remains of my garden. The woman in the midst of it has on a gown that could easily be confounded with the greenery. Upon closer inspection, I can see roots and vines entwined across her body, almost like a darker precursor, a reminder of her power.

Yet her expression, when she notices me, is radiant. "Hades."

She opens her arms, and I step closer. Pulling her into a hug, I inhale her scent of cloves and spices, mixed with something earthy. I pull back, and sparkling eyes the color of the moon meet mine.

"Morrigan." Ruler of the Celts. Head of her own pantheon. And a long-time friend of mine.

She glances over my shoulder, and I hasten to reassure her. "That's Ileana, my immortal guardian. I trust her."

"Ah, yes. We all have one of those these days."

I arch an eyebrow. "Even you?"

Something moves out of the shadows. He could be her brother, and while I would have thought him as arrogant as Frumos, a kind of gentleness escapes him. With one nod from her, he steps back into the shadows, hiding once more. Ileana follows suit and does the same, leaving us alone to chat.

"What's happening, Morrigan? The Council meeting, Odin… I can't have missed that much."

She laughs. "You did spend a lot of time inebriated these last centuries… But, no, you did not. What is afoot has been underfoot, so to speak, for a while."

"And what is it?"

For the first time, her expression falters. "You have to understand, this is but speculation on my end."

I should have figured out as much. Otherwise, she would have brought it up to Zeus himself and the Council.

"Whatever takes place, it may have started with the Norse gods, but it will affect us all, in the end. Something evil has been unleashed."

"Evil?" A sigh escapes me. "Is this about me speaking Old Tongue again?"

Morrigan wrings her hands, looking past me again. "Not quite, no. This has to do with an *entity* of evil. I do not know the details, nor whether it is one of ours, yours, or theirs."

"You mean whether it's one of the abominations we fought, way back?"

"Yes. You had the Titans, we had more. We thought those evils vanquished, imprisoned for good. But where we—each pantheon—have them locked up, it is not enough. Those walls are shaking, and more are escaping. I believe that is what possessed Fenrir, and he did not know who you were."

So I *did* miss something. And Zeus, as usual, is wrong about this being related to politics. While I can't reveal to Morrigan what I heard from Fenrir—that would amount to explaining more than that—I can help ease her thoughts.

"I did get a sense something was... wrong...with him."

Morrigan nods. "Too much. We believe it also caused him to turn against his own pantheon, and to actually hurt them."

That's not good, not in the least. And if he's being affected, how many others will follow suit? And *what* is causing this mess?

"Where is he now?"

"No one knows. But, we are hunting for him."

I shake my head. "Morrigan, this is...

You have to tell Zeus."

"Your brother has his own ideas of what is causing this."

"Meaning?" My feint doesn't fool her.

She tilts her head to the side, as if I should know better. And, in a way, I do. He was already very clear. There is only one thing he has ever cared for, and that is being ruler of Olympus. The Council has seen his leadership, meaning he will soon get his wish.

"Of course," I say, giving up all pretense. "He thinks someone is doing it to stop him from achieving full control." Her faint nod is enough confirmation. "What can I do?"

"If you know of anyone traveling the realms, stop them. Nothing is safe, not until we all lay our cards on the table and work together."

If we can even get to that…

I try not to focus on her thoughts as she hugs me, but it's hard. Morrigan has stayed more in tune with other pantheons than we have, and she's off next to visit the Egyptians.

"Good luck," I whisper.

She pulls away with an odd look. "With?"

Shit. I'm really getting careless. "With, uh…

I'm assuming you're going to warn others?"

"You know me so well."

I force a smile, and then she's gone in a flurry of dark green smoke.

Ileana, quick as always, has a portal waiting. "I assume you wish to get Persephone?"

"How did you...?"

"You are not the only one who can read minds." She jumps in, ignoring my baffled expression, and I have no choice but to follow.

I stumble out of the portal, moving in front of Ileana to block her way.

"What do you mean, *read minds*?" How did she figure it out? And who will she tell?

My heart thuds at a faster pace. I'm more afraid than I have been in a while. More aware, too. My palms are clammy, something I haven't experienced since I was a young deity, and my teeth are gritted so hard I'm worried they might snap. And still, my gaze is inflexible on Ileana.

She smiles like she holds a secret, then brushes some imaginary dirt off my shirt. "I know, Hades."

"How? Do you also—"

"Nu." Her brilliant gaze catches mine. "I am not gifted such as you are, but it does not take a genius to figure it out. Not when you wear your emotions on your sleeve as you do."

"I do not!"

"I beg to differ. We can continue discussing this later, but for now, we must find your love interest."

I shove all the questions I have aside and focus on that one thing.

This time, now that I know what I'm looking for—and I haven't had ambrosia for a few hours—I find Persephone easily. When she sees me nearing, she steps away from the human she was speaking to. Her expression is anything but welcoming.

I follow her around a house and find her leaning against it. Her chin is tilted in the air, arms crossed over her chest, her expression defiant. Her eyes flicker to Ileana, behind me, then narrow on me.

"What do you want this time?"

"You're not safe here."

She rolls her eyes. "Consider me warned. Is that all?"

When she tries to move, I grab her elbow to stop her. It's the second time I've touched her without her permission, but I can't seem to stop myself. And while another goddess would have zapped me into obedience by now, she does not.

It would be even more interesting if I can hear her thoughts—which still elude me, sadly.

"Persephone, please. Listen to me."

"I *am* listening. You, however, aren't. I don't wish to go anywhere, and I'm perfectly fine here."

I tug her farther away, ignoring her protests. She is incensed once I find us a corner for more privacy. "You aren't taking this seriously enough."

"Nor should I. I'm safe, and I would love it if you could stop pretending you care. You've seen me, twice. Since when is that enough to make you care?"

I open my mouth to deny it—and point

out this is technically my third time, but then again the quick flash I'd seen of her the first time could've been a trick of my mind. And, either way, what can I say? That I've been dreaming of her laugh for weeks, to the point of being addicted? That I know the smell of her hair, and fall asleep with her scent in my nostrils, even though I've only been around her a few times?

Not smooth enough. Why didn't I listen when Zeus tried to give me pointers?

And then it dawns on me. Maybe she's not here by her own accord. After all, what goddess of Olympus would choose the earthly realm over ours?

"Is someone keeping you here, against your will?" My imagination runs haywire, especially given what Morrigan told me… "If anyone's—"

Persephone yanks herself out of my grip and shoves me away. "No! I *choose* to be here. Is that so hard to understand, that I'd rather be among humans who value me for who I am, rather than what I am and what I can or cannot do?"

"I—"

Her outburst shocks me, but not as much as the tears filling her eyes. What kind of minefield have I just stepped in?

"Leave." It's a near growl, her eyes throwing darts my way. "I'm happy here, and you're ruining it for me."

And not for the first time, she walks away from me.

CHAPTER SEVEN

"That went well."

I ignore Ileana and turn to the party, getting lost in the throng of people. But not for long. Even as I get a mug of ale, she's on my heels. Her radiant self attracts more than one eye, so I grab her forearm and tug her down in a corner table.

"Could you be a little less conspicuous?"

She glances around, notices a few stares, and nods. As soon as the humans look away, her form becomes less shimmery, less bright, and she seems almost…human. Approachable. Until one sees the glint of coolness in her eyes— but no humans would get close enough.

"That'll do," I mutter and bury my nose in the jug.

Ileana wrinkles her nose but says nothing. I ignore her obvious disapproval and drink the entire thing, followed by another. Still, she keeps silent, watching me get wasted on cheap beer that will most likely give me indigestion as earthly goods usually do.

"Not saying anything?"

"I have long since given hope of keeping you sober, Hades."

I glare at her but push the drink away — momentarily, at least. "Why's that?"

"Because you seem to take great pleasure in diminishing yourself."

"Excuse me?"

She delivers the words so carelessly, so indifferently, my ego takes a hit.

"Is it any wonder Persephone wants nothing to do with you?"

Low blow. "You should recall you're speaking to a god, Ileana. And while I may be unable to release you from your duties, I could take great pleasure in making them much, much worse."

She jerks, as if surprised by the venom in

my voice. She's not alone. I always thought out of the three of us, Zeus was the one more stuck-up and filled with arrogance. *Guess I was wrong.*

Ileana stares me down, then looks away. After what we've shared so far, and the fact I've come to see her as a friend, I would expect at least a fight. Something to bring me down a peg, to call me out on my bullshit. Instead, I get nothing. No frown, no expression whatsoever, other than a complete dismissal.

The rest of the night, she stands by and watches me drink myself into a stupor—in as much as a god can, which is not much.

And all along, I'm keeping an eye out for Persephone. Waiting for her to return, but too proud to seek her and find out more. Her words haunt me. What did she mean, she gets more out of humans here than the gods at home?

And, more to the point, can I really pretend I don't know what she means by that, when I myself have sought refuge among humans multiple times?

The mugs of ale stack up on the table,

and still Ileana says nothing.

When the night passes and I've grown bored and weary of the events, she drags me back home through a portal. The rest is all darkness…

I wake the next morning with another dull ache in my head. Ileana is nowhere to be seen, and Frumos is in a sour mood. Two days go by in such silence, and it's enough to make my teeth grind. Especially given the silence isn't mental. No, in their own heads, both of my guards have plenty to say. Ileana continues to stay away, and it dawns on me that while I was busy snoring away, she filled Frumos in on what I'd said.

The last thing I'd wanted was to hurt her or cause this tension. But now that I have, my pride won't let me undo it. The same way it doesn't let me undo it by asking Persephone for forgiveness for the way I'd acted, for my presumptions, and adding stress on her.

In retrospect, I now realize trying to tell

a goddess of Olympus what to do was idiotic at best. Incredibly harming at worst. But my stupid mouth ran off without me. And after all, I *am* the black sheep of Olympus. I may not know who she is, but she must know that, at least.

On the third day of my sour mood, I pull myself out of bed and get dressed, then pivot to Frumos. Ileana, as per the last few days, is gone again.

"Are you any good with that sword, immortal?" I ask him.

When us gods retired from the world of humans, that left us with few things to do. Most of us got bored and drew to vices. And then, some of us kept certain good habits. It has been a while since I've focused on mine.

Frumos looks up from a scroll he'd been reading. "Da, of course."

"Good. Then you can entertain me today."

Without explaining myself, I walk out of my area of the palace, stomping about with purpose. Rather than use the convenient portals, I take the stairs and go down the four flights of our mansion, before heading out toward the manicured lawn. I bypass it, knowing Frumos is following me, and instead continue onward until I find us a quiet spot by a stream.

Something must be going on for Olympus to be this empty, but I don't really pay it attention. I'm too filled with energy I need to let go of.

Where in all hells is he taking me?

I ignore his question and instead face Frumos, gesturing to the area. "This should do." I reach out, divine energy rushing through me. In my hands, I materialize a sword.

Frumos stares at me a second, then reaches into the fold of air itself. His hand shimmers, then out comes a different sword. Its blade attracts some rays of light. *Damascus steel. How intriguing.* These immortals keep surprising me.

He twirls the weapon in his grip, his eyes narrowing on my form. "Not the first time you've done this?"

"You could say that."

I attack before he can, determined to get some of the steam out of me. He blocks me without a problem. I return to my original position, as he does. We're mirror images of each other, left leg leading, swords held with both hands to the left shoulder, weight carried on the back leg. A trickle of competitiveness runs up my spine, and I grin.

Frumos side-steps to the right and brings his sword down, but I parry it at the perfect angle. Metal clangs as our blades clash.

"Not bad for a lazy god," he says.

"Lazy?"

The jab has the desired effect, and I launch faster at him. Only, it seems we've both underestimated each other. For each of my parries, Frumos meets them and pushes me back. Each time I destabilize him, he brings me down with him.

"Are you this angry because of what I said to Ileana?" I ask in between strikes.

The quality of his lashing out changes, becoming even more determined. His jaw clenches. *Shouldn't have talked to her like that. But what did I expect from an Olympian?*

"I was not even there," he says out loud. "What is there to be angry about?"

"Something's gotten up your butt, then."

He laughs. "Of course you would believe that. Everything has to be about you." His next attack is a bit too close to hurting me, but I move out of the way. "Have you ever considered that not everything revolves around you Olympians?"

What is it about these immortals that so easily gets under my skin? Perhaps it's the fact they see me, and they don't pretend otherwise. Instead, they make it a point to call me on my shit and force me into self-reflection.

Like Ileana did. Unwelcome, but also a wake-up call. How utterly...annoying. And destabilizing.

For once in my pitiful existence, I can't bury myself in ambrosia. With a jolt, I realize I've barely had any the last few days, instead replacing that with sleeping. And thinking. Too much damned thinking.

Gods don't self-reflect. They act. They do. They take. They...exist. To be faced with these creatures, it's unsettling.

I hide my thoughts under another attack. Frumos parries too fast, and the sword nearly nicks my neck—I lean backward, and all it does is cut my shirt. I scowl at him.

Ileana chooses that moment to burst in,

eyes narrowed on our swords. "Are you two done being idiots?"

There's a chill in the air around her, even more so when she looks at Frumos. Or, rather, at a point above his head. Perhaps this has nothing to do with me, after all. Did I sleep through something interesting?

"Is this really a good idea?" Frumos asks the minute we're out of the portal.

It took me the better part of another day to convince Frumos to accompany me to the human realm again. After our little parry lesson, and more self-reflection, I figured I had to at least try again with Persephone. It's not like I can get her out of my mind. So, either I go insane—more than I already am—or I bite the bullet and talk to her.

"How do you even know she will be here?" Frumos asks.

"I don't."

Not true. I do, because I dreamed of her again last night. *Her* being Persephone.

"Why did I even bother asking?" he mutters.

I stop in my tracks and glower at him. "Are you done being annoyed at me? You can't really protect me if you hate me."

He scowls. "I do not hate you. I hate what you represent and how arrogant you are. Even for a deity."

"Clearly, you haven't been around my brother enough."

"Nor do I wish it. Or Ileana."

I run a hand over my face. "I *am* sorry for what I said to her."

"It is not me you should be apologizing to."

"Fair enough."

And I will. Soon as I find Persephone and talk to her again. Just…once. I'll make sure when I walk away today, it'll be the last time. It has to be. I can't be spending my days chasing vixens, it'd make me no better than Zeus.

Soon as I stop focusing on Frumos, thoughts of humans assail me. I try to block them off, seeking the one person I'm here to find. And, sure enough, her laughter draws me in.

"Steady." Frumos grabs my arm and holds me back. "Take in the surroundings first."

I ignore the jab—a poor reference to our previous sparring session—and instead do as he demands. Persephone is holding court, probably not even realizing it. Couples, and single humans, are hanging on to her every word.

She hasn't yet seen me, which gives me a perfect chance to watch her, without doing anything. And that's when I notice it again. Under all the radiance, under all the smiles, there's a darkness there. Her words from before echo in my mind. *Is that so hard to understand, that I'd rather be among humans who value me for who I am, rather than what I am and what I can or cannot do?*

I didn't bother listening to her, then. But now, I do. Whatever demons are haunting her, whatever her reason to be here, is it truly my right to interfere?

I don't know how long I spend watching her. Conflicted. Undecided. Finally, after long enough, I pivot to Frumos and meet his stunned expression. "Let's go."

"Zeus sends word," Ileana surprises me that night by saying. It's just the two of us, since Frumos went on some errand or other. "The Council will reconvene at sundown."

"Now you're talking to me?" I can't help the childish comment.

She hasn't said a word for days, unless absolutely necessary, and it's aggravating. Mainly because I know I must apologize. And I still haven't.

Ileana shrugs and turns her back on me.

"Did he say anything else?"

"No."

I wait for more, but it never comes. At least, not until I head toward the decanter of ambrosia.

I would've thought you heard enough from my thoughts.

I freeze and slowly pivot, narrowing my eyes on her expression. Eyebrows arched, arms folded over her chest, she seems expectant. And, why not?

That's yet another thing we never truly

addressed. How she knew about my abilities, how she figured me out in days when I've eluded most deities.

A sigh escapes me. "When did you know, exactly?"

"That you can hear thoughts? After the first Council meeting, for sure. Before that? I had my suspicions."

"Does Frumos know?"

"Not from me. But, he has mentioned your odd behavior."

I shake my head. "I don't get it. For eons, most of Olympus couldn't figure me out. And you two come along, and already you see more than everyone else."

Ileana shrugs. "Our duty is to watch you. We are bound to."

"Ah." I take a gulp of the ambrosia. "Well, then, I am sorry, about what I said that night. And how I said it. I was frustrated at all you could see."

"Thank you. But to be clear, I do not take anything I said back."

"I figured as much. Nor do I expect you to. And yes, you are correct about my inability to stay away from alcohol, ambrosia, the vices.

But what you may have missed is I do this to numb the voices."

"I did not miss it. But are there no better ways?"

How to explain what I have been going through, without sounding like a whiny child and the loner I am? There's no way.

Frumos chooses that moment to step through the door, sparing me. "They're reconvening now."

I nod and follow them out the door. Time to dive into some more useless chatter.

Perhaps I'll get lucky and Persephone will come to me.

CHAPTER EIGHT

Pegasus bounds up next to me as I'm waiting outside the atrium. We're all lined up like cattle—deities from all pantheons—waiting to get inside. Since we're practically magnets together, him and me, he has no issue finding me. Plus, my glowing immortal guards make me an easy target. For the first time, I realize that not all immortals have them, and those who do, have various colored glows.

I turn to Frumos. "What's with the glows around you guys?"

"Different personalities," he mutters.

I glance between him and Ileana meaningfully. "That why you two are so much the same?"

She snorts, he clenches his jaw, and that's the end of it.

Wow. Whatever happened with them must be worse than I thought. Or better.

Pegasus nudges me, interrupting my thoughts. "Have you heard?"

"What?"

"Zeus officially won his bid for Olympus. The conclave relented to his ideas, he had undivided support. He'll be supreme ruler before we know it."

"Good for him."

I didn't hear, nor do I care. He's my brother, but there is nothing left between us other than disdain and contempt. More on his part than mine. For my end, I would be perfectly happy if he chose to forget my very existence.

Not likely.

Pegasus watches me intently. *I would've thought he'd have more of a reaction. How long has it been since Zeus held this over his head?*

Long enough. Since Zeus found out just how different I am, all he's done is hold his aspirations over my head and use them to berate me. *If you make me lose this… If they start thinking I'm as crazy as you are… You're my brother, you should have my best interests at heart…* And on it went.

I've learned to ignore it, these last centuries. Ambrosia has helped, as has my ability to get out of Olympus. Not anymore, I guess.

To add to it, it's getting harder and harder to ignore thoughts. To avoid saying what I truly wish to say, responding directly. So instead of giving in to the trap with Pegasus, I focus on the crowd. There are more deities than before in the atrium, and we're packed shoulder to shoulder. Word must have gotten out about the in-fighting.

And still, I keep seeking. Last time, I wasn't aware of Persephone's identity. Now I am. Surely, she should be somewhere here, listening in?

"What are you looking for?"

"Not what. Who."

Pegasus arches an eyebrow. "Someone I know?"

"Maybe…" It occurs to me, had I been less proud, I could've gotten an answer to my question a while ago from him. "Persephone?"

Pegasus frowns. "You mean, Demeter's daughter?"

Demeter! That's why she was familiar... I remember a youthful, carefree goddess. Her mother sits on the conclave that's been in Zeus' way for eons. My memories of her are few and sparse between—probably an indication of the centuries I've spent completely drunk.

But how would she have ended among humans? Why would she prefer them to our kind? Something tells me Demeter didn't allow her daughter to part merrily. After all, I recall in Demeter a fierce goddess with an iron fist. Not someone easily swayed.

"Yes, her," I mutter.

Pegasus tilts his head to the side. He knows me too well and sees past my short reply. "How did you run into her?"

"Does it matter?"

"Yes." His eyes shine with amusement. "It has been a long, long, *long*—"

"I get it!"

"—time since I've last seen you so, hmm, invested."

"I'm not invested."

And there he goes again with the petulant

attitude, Ileana thinks behind me. I throw her a glare over my shoulder just so she knows I heard her. Her smile tells me that was the intent all along.

In an effort to avoid a full-on conversation with her, I let out a low growl and focus on Pegasus. "Remember the woman I was seeking, at the last party we went to?"

Pegasus nods. "Among the humans?"

"Yes. That was Persephone. She just… caught my attention, is all."

He chuckles and slaps my back. "Whatever you say, brother. Well, to answer you, yes, I do know her, but you should save your efforts. She never comes to these things."

"Why?"

He shrugs. "Bit of a recluse, or so they say. Overbearing mom and all."

Pegasus *would* know, he's aware of everything going on in here.

"And…" He trails off, but at my expectant expression, finishes with, "There are rumors something's wrong with her."

I recall the darkness I'd felt. Overshadowing her radiance, once I caught on to it. Could the rest of the deities be aware of that, too? Is that why she doesn't want to be in Olympus?

At a loss, I ask, "Like what?"

"Not showing a proficiency of powers. She's meant to be spring personified, but the last party Zeus gave, she couldn't make a single flower blossom."

Something about that image rings a bell. Enough to make me uneasy. "Was I at that party?"

Pegasus gives me an odd look. "Of course. You're the one who suggested she provide entertainment." When I say nothing, he adds, "By showcasing her powers."

I stumble back at his words, delivered in an indifferent tone. Frumos steadies me with his hand on my shoulder, while Pegasus frowns at me.

Frumos' touch has the unwelcome effect of drilling his thoughts straight into my mind. *...and now she won't talk to me? Insane. Why must all women act so sensitive over things that we men don't even overthink? How could I have known she was still touchy about —*

I yank myself out of his grip, stumbling into another god.

He glares at me. "Go drink somewhere

else, Hades. No one needs you here."

I clench my fist, trying to stifle the anger rising inside me. There are too many people around, too many things that can go wrong, but all I want in that moment is a chance to finally let loose some of the energy driving me crazy.

Hades.

My gaze snaps to Ileana's.

"Breathe," she mouths. *Take a deep breath before you have another attack. Zeus will not like it.*

I listen to her and do as she demands. Then my thoughts focus back on the whole reason for my reaction. Persephone.

I'd rather be among humans who value me for who I am, rather than what I am and what I can or cannot do.

Is that why? She left Olympus because of my callous attitude? My stomach rolls at the thought, especially given what I've endured these last centuries. And that was without Olympians even knowing the true reason I act so differently. But if they did...

I owe her a massive apology.

And then some.

The last thing I want to do is be stuck in an atrium with so many thoughts around me. But I can't *not* go. Aside from Zeus asking me to spy on Odin, I also need to figure out how dangerous all this can be for us. For Persephone.

The atrium doors open, and we all storm inside. I grab Pegasus' arm and meet his gaze. "Go to Persephone. Please. She's in the same village I was attacked, you can't miss her. Please, go to her."

"What? Why?" He glances to the open area, evidently wanting to be in there instead.

"I'll come find you as soon as this is done. But for me, brother, please do it. Just keep an eye on her until I get there."

Pegasus stares at me for another beat, then smiles and nods. "All right, but I expect all the details." Then he turns his back on me and takes off. At the edge of the building, he's surrounded by a shimmering, rainbow-colored light, and his body morphs to the white-winged horse I know.

"Hades."

Ileana and Frumos are on either side of the doors, waiting for me to follow. And beyond them is Zeus, his expectant glare on me. I nod, enough to tell him I haven't forgotten his orders.

I move inside, and my guards fall in step with me. We find a spot next to one of the columns, in full view of Zeus and Odin.

Moments later, Zeus calls everyone to order, and the cacophony lowers to murmurs. The thoughts are another story, but I do my best to waive them away mentally.

Odin stands, leaning on a staff. He settles his good eye on my brother. "We are unable to produce Fenrir at this moment, as per your request."

Zeus' expression is thunderous. "There better be a good reason for it."

Odin shares a look with the other gods. Besides my brother, everyone else holds their tongue. But suspicion fills their thoughts, assailing me once more.

He had one task, and one alone.

The Norse were responsible for our last issues…

I give my head a small shake, trying to concentrate.

"We cannot find him," Odin says. "In fact, we fear something worse has happened."

Zeus waves a hand dismissively. "Or, he's simply gone rogue."

This fool — Odin takes a deep breath. He is older than us, and my brother should not be irritating him to this extent, not that he cares.

After a long moment, Odin says, "Fenrir would not do so. He is a dear friend of mine, and my son's."

I focus on the two men accompanying him. One is Thor, who I've seen before, but the other is his exact opposite. Smaller, with dark hair and an angular face. Oddly, the dark-haired one seems to feel my gaze on him and stares back in open interest.

Loki.

I peek over my shoulder at Ileana, arching an eyebrow in silent question. *Is that his name?*

Not someone you want to engage with. Especially you, she warns.

I give a slight nod to indicate I'll listen.

Zeus stands from his chair, moving around. "We only have your word to count on."

Odin leans forward. "Are you implying it is not enough?"

I can't be the only one noticing the pure wrath in his voice, nor the way the ground itself seems to shudder.

Zeus stops, all his attention on Odin. *Oh no.* I know that look. I've seen it plenty of times, directed at me. And if no one stops him, he's going to—

Morrigan intervenes. "He is most definitely not, great Odin. Let us try to find a solution to this. May I propose something?" When Zeus nods, albeit reluctantly, she continues, "If you are afraid something has happened to Fenrir, you may not be wrong."

A snort from Loki follows her words. Thor elbows him, nearly sending him sprawling on the floor, but Loki falls silent. I don't know why I find him so interesting. Perhaps because he, too, seems so far removed from this situation, like me?

Then I recall I'm supposed to be listening to his father's inner musings. Reluctantly, I aim my gaze to Odin.

The moment I connect with his energy, the same one that flows through us all, his thoughts become my own. *I cannot tell them everything. Loki is correct, the Olympians will only use this situation to turn everyone against us. We cannot lose more ground than we have. Not if—*

Someone clears their throat behind me. I pivot to Ileana, but it's not me she's staring at. No, her glower is concentrated on Loki. Whose scrutiny, it seems, I've attracted with my shenanigans on his father.

Whatever it is you are doing, Ileana thinks at me, *stop it. Loki is too interested in you right now.*

I guess Zeus will have to make do with what I've found. Which is basically nothing.

"What do you suggest, Morrigan of the Celts?" Odin says after a long pause.

"We all have immortal guards at this stage. And we have taken these precautions because we have all, without exception, witnessed odd happenings in our own realms. Perhaps we can take a few days to see where our evils are hidden, and ensure we are not missing any. Any that could be…dangerous …to all."

A longer silence falls, even on the crowds. Everyone is waiting.

Then Zeus nods. "Very well. Let us meet back in a fortnight."

No sooner is the Council done than I storm out with my immortal guards. "I need to get back to the humans."

"Do you think it wise, given what just took place in there?" Ileana hisses.

Frumos clears his throat. At first I think it's because of how close she is to me, then I realize his attention is on someone else. Zeus. And his presence behind me.

Biting back a groan, I face my brother's stormy expression. Too late, I catch on that his gaze is narrowed on me and Ileana.

"You have time for cavorting when my fate is in danger?"

"Melodrama doesn't suit you, brother." I roll my eyes. "And I much prefer leaving the cavorting to you."

He ignores me, instead taking a step closer. "Tell me."

I glance over his shoulder, trailing with my eyes Loki, Thor, and Odin as they depart. My voice is but a whisper when I say, "Odin knows more than he says. But I could not pick up what, exactly, is wrong. Morrigan's suggestion seems best at this stage."

Zeus clenches his jaw. "As usual, you're

utterly useless. Thanks for nothing, *brother*."

He stomps away, and I do my best to shake off his ugly words.

I think Morrigan was right all along, and there is something much, much bigger going on here. But I'm not about to risk waiting to find out, not when I have amends to do.

A few deep breaths later, I pivot to my guards. "What just happened in there doesn't matter. You can either come with me, or not."

They share a look, and Ileana nods. She seems to have gotten over her earlier coolness around Frumos. "You go. I will try to find out more information about what has taken place, to ensure we are not blindsided."

A few moments later, we emerge out of a portal again into the village. It's daytime on Earth, and the village is empty as most humans go about their daily chores. I seek Persephone but don't find her anywhere close.

Frumos on my heels, I head off into the fields. If she's anywhere, I would imagine it is around there. Sure enough, I find her amid some women, picking berries and laughing with them.

Watching her, the way she carries herself,

does something to me. I've never been part of the gods who fall non-stop for other goddesses and bed them. Doesn't mean I haven't had trysts, but it is what it is. With Persephone, something else draws me in. She's so kind with humans, so grounded...

Perhaps that's a big part of it. She, like my guards, constantly calls me out on my bullshit. And, of course, there's the fact I need to know why she's not adding to the chaos in my mind.

Sensing eyes on her, she stops her conversation and studies her surroundings. Her violet gaze finally settles on me a few moments later.

I'm not sure what to expect—will she get annoyed, seeing me here again, or will she come and talk to me?

After a moment of hesitation, she chooses the latter. Basket of berries on her hip, she steps over to me, and I don't look away the entire time. As soon as she's only a foot away, her scent wafting to me, the voices in my head—and Frumos' incessant monologue—cease.

"Hello, Hades."

CHAPTER NINE

"Persephone."

My mouth is weirdly dry when I try to answer. In an effort to hide my unease, I grab a mug of ale from a passing human and take a big gulp. Frumos stands to the side.

"Well?"

"Well, what?"

Her expression becomes amused. "You've been watching me for a while. First your friend, now you?"

"My fri—"

Pegasus bounds out of the fields then, a broad grin on his face. "Sorry. She saw me within moments."

"Ah." I run a hand over my neck, struggling to explain it to her—the utter panic that she might be in danger, when I've only seen her a handful of times and have instead contributed to making her life hell in Olympus.

He did not think this through, Frumos thinks, and I want to slam my fist in his face. But I don't, only in my mind.

I clear my throat. "My apologies about that."

She shrugs. "Not like my mother hasn't done the same. And, at least Pegasus here was fun enough to offer to pick berries with me." She points to her basket. "Want some?"

"No, thank you."

I glance between them, trying to ignore the flash of jealousy running through me. How can she be so comfortable with him when she's been shunning me away?

Oh, right. Because he didn't out her to all Olympians and make her feel inferior.

"Why?"

I blink. "Sorry?"

"Why send your best friend to watch over me?"

"Just…" I give up all pretense and instead

jerk my head to one of the darker corners, away from humans. "Could I have your attention, for a moment? Just the two of us?"

Her gaze goes to Frumos over my shoulder.

"He'll wait here." My order is meant more for his ears than hers.

Persephone hesitates again, then nods and leads the way. My gaze is drawn to the movements of her body as she walks ahead of me. And much as I try to drag my thoughts from it and what it would feel like under mine, I can't help them. I feel a weird urge to just…hold her. Feel her hand in mine. Her lips.

"What is it you wish to talk to me about?" She stops so abruptly, I nearly bump into her.

"Come back to Olympus." *Smooth. Very smooth.*

Wariness fills her gaze. "Hades, did I not already say—"

"To leave you alone, yes. I get that. But there are desperate things at play here."

"Like what?"

"When was the last time you saw your mother?"

Her expression shuts down. "You don't know me well enough to ask me that."

"You're correct." Not the right time to bring up my own faux pas. Or is it the perfect one? As it stands, I'm a coward, and cowards run away from problems. "But, please. Consider returning to Olympus. There is something going on with the gods, across all pantheons. And it's leading to evil escaping, perhaps even to us being hunted."

"Then I'm safest here."

"What do you mean?"

"No one will look for me among humans. Believe me."

I want to admire her sauciness, her grit, but instead, only darkness feeds my soul. "Persephone, please—"

"No. Thank you for your concern, but *no*."

I grasp her wrist before she passes me.

She glances down at it. "You seem to be making a habit of grabbing me."

"Should I apologize?"

Something sparks in her gaze. Not desire, per se, but intrigue. A bit of lust, or is that wishful thinking on my part? Her lips part, and then she pulls herself out of my grip. "Another time, perhaps."

Once she's gone, Frumos comes back to

me. "Ready to return to Olympus?'

"No."

"Is it not odd behavior to stick around, when she clearly does not want you?"

"Maybe, but do you see an immortal guard with her?"

Frumos won't say, but I'm clearly right. So, I don't make a move for a portal, instead I dive back into the throng of humans. To keep an eye on her, for as long as she'll let me.

A week passes by, while I sneak in the human town, sleeping under the stars, and keep an eye on Persephone. Frumos gets more annoyed with every passing moment, and Pegasus comes by more than once, trying to lure me back home.

Nothing works. I'm a man possessed. Day in and day out, I watch Persephone. From what I can gather, she's some sort of healer here. Humans drift around her like bees to honey, and there is no fear of her abilities. Here, among them, the little magic she has is enough to make them worship her. In Olympus, it only leads to shunning.

Which brings me again to what I did and how my callous actions messed up her existence. The more I watch over Persephone, the more I see that same darkness in her. And I realize it's not all that much different than mine. And still, her thoughts elude me.

Unlike Frumos'. It's nighttime, there's another party in town, and as I stand just on the edge, him by my side, he won't shut up. *There has to a way to get him back to Olympus. This is bordering on obsession.*

I scowl at him, jabbing a finger in his face. "Stay back this time. I want to speak with Persephone alone."

Without waiting for his response, I approach her. She rolls her eyes when she sees me. She's only dancing, but I move past the human and take hold of her waist, twirling her around to the tune.

"I know why you dislike me."

"Really?" Her eyes widen, though she doesn't miss a beat. In truth, she's keeping up with the music much more than I am.

"A few centuries ago, I put you on the

spot during one of Zeus' parties."

She tries to stop dancing, but I only tighten my hold. The movement pulls her closer against me, forcing her to continue, lest we both fall.

"It was humiliating, especially when you couldn't produce the kind of magic us gods are known for. I need to apologize for that."

Persephone stares away, trying to put space between us once more. I don't let go. It feels too good, having her in my arms, much better than dreaming of her.

"I'm sorry. I'm doubly sorry for taking this long to apologize."

She stares at me for a beat, the violet hue in her eyes almost blazing in the torchlight. I feel the weight of her gaze to my bones. And the relief at finally giving her what she is owed.

"It was a long time ago," she finally says.

"But it still hurt. And, perhaps, contributed to you not being in Olympus so much anymore."

Her mouth falls slightly open, and a shocked burst of laughter escapes her. I'm both enchanted at being the object of her amusement, and annoyed. Especially when she adds, "You think too highly of yourself, Hades."

"No. I'm simply used to wearing a mask, too."

She searches my expression, trying to see what I'm thinking. She won't be able to, not unless I allow her. And, can I? If she goes and tells everyone else what she sees, as a way to get back at me, I will be screwed in more ways than one.

But if she doesn't…

I hold my breath and let my usual neutrality fall, allowing her to see the loneliness, the isolation, the differences.

Persephone stops dancing for good this time, as do I. We're unable to tear our gazes apart, until someone bumps into me from behind, crashing me into her. When I steady her and pull back, our faces are inches apart. Too close. Much too close, much too soon.

And yet she surprises me by taking a stride closer and brushing our lips together.

Then she pushes me away, her eyes widening. "I don't know why I did that."

"I do."

"No, you really don't."

In a flash, she's gone again.

Frumos appears by my side a moment later, his look as morose as they come.

"What happened to you?" I ask him.

"Ileana came by while you were busy."

"Had a spat?"

He blows out a breath. "As we always seem to."

I gesture around. "Well, I've been abandoned once more. I say a better course of action for us tonight is to stay away from females, and instead do what human men do when in trouble."

"Which is?"

"Drown our sorrows in alcohol."

Frumos grins. "A perfect plan."

In retrospect, perhaps getting drunk wasn't the best idea. Especially not with everything else going on. But, I thought I could handle it. Until some human men joined the party and brought loads of heavy liquor.

Within hours, Frumos and I were out of our minds. Sobriety would enter our streams soon enough, but for the time being, we were out of the village and sitting on a hill overlooking it.

"Are you and Ileana lovers?" I ask him abruptly.

"Why?" *What does he want with her? Does he not have enough with Persephone?*

I try to hold back a laugh at his panicked thoughts. They're less collected than normal, almost youthful now that he's drunk. Not for the first time, I wonder just how old him and Ileana are.

"I'm not trying to encroach on your territory, breathe. Simple curiosity."

My reassuring seems to help him, as he nods. "We had a brief encounter, when in immortal school together. About two hundred years ago."

My jaw drops. "Two *hundred*? How long is your training, exactly?"

Frumos shrugs. "About that length. Some of us are assigned to deities alone, but others as a pair. We only find out at the end of the training, when our respective mentors give us our assignments. In our case, we did not know such would be the fate for us, hence the... friction."

"A little more than friction, I'd say."

Frumos is quiet, playing with some twigs of grass.

"So two hundred years ago, you two had a thing going. How, exactly?"

"The usual way. I was out seeking some fun, to make up for a dreadful day I'd had. She was out practicing her defensive magic." His voice lowers, almost to a whisper. "I offered to teach her. She was always so put together, and seeing her that frustrated, that vulnerable, did something to me. Neither of us were supposed to feel, but that night, perhaps because of everything we had forced ourselves *not* to feel, it all came out. And...it imploded my world, in a way I did not expect." A humorless laugh escapes him. "Ileana chose to ignore it, saying she was focused on completing her training and becoming the best guardian she can be. One that legends would be written about."

"Mm, yes, she does seem driven. And you?"

"I think there was more than a one-night

stand, and I have been trying to convince her of that. Ever since."

It's my turn to appear surprised. "When? I haven't heard you arguing."

"And yet you spend so much time awake… not."

Ah. "Point taken. So, you have all your heavy conversations once I'm out of commission."

He shrugs.

"And what caused this particular spat?"

"You."

"How so?"

"She knows something about you that could give me a better understanding of how to protect you. But she will not trust me enough to tell me."

Doesn't take a genius to figure out what the *something* is. A heavy sigh escapes me. "It's because it's not her secret to tell."

"I realize as much, yet I need to know."

I watch him out of the corner of my eye, observing his profile. As if sensing my gaze, he meets it with a frown. Not too long ago, I was thinking of sharing this secret with Persephone. Now, I'm debating on sharing it with him. A guard whose favor I most definitely have not earned.

The words are out of my mouth before I can stop them. "I can read thoughts."

"You… What?"

"Since I was born. All gods are born with perfect bodies and minds, yet mine got warped somehow. I can hear everyone's thoughts, have been able to for as long as I can remember."

Frumos takes it all in, shock all over his expression, from the wide eyes to the slack jaw. "But Olympus, they have no idea?"

"No. And I want to keep it that way."

Frumos nods. I imagine his training kicks in, as he pulls him together rather fast. "I understand. I may not get it to that extent but… They will not find out from me. You have my word."

Oddly, I believe him. And I also trust that him and Ileana will keep my secret safe — but would Persephone?

When I say nothing, just focus on watching the village again, he adds, "Why tell me?"

"Because it's not necessary for you two to suffer due to my mistakes."

"Back again?"

"I am."

After revealing my secret to Frumos, I sent him back to Olympus. Ileana returned moments later, her expression a little less angry and a lot more grateful. So, when I told her I wanted to go talk to Persephone again, she didn't object.

She's waiting somewhere in the shadows now, giving me a moment, and keeping an eye out while I desperately try not to screw up again.

I take a deep breath. "You didn't listen to me last time."

Persephone runs a hand over her face. "I did. Something about a danger you cannot name, but that's supposed to get me back to Olympus."

"Walk with me."

"No."

"Persephone…"

"What gives you the right to start interfering here? I've told you off already. I'm not interested in being rescued."

"This has nothing to do with being rescued."

"Really?" She looks me up and down. "So you being a big, bad god isn't related?"

No words come out of my mouth. Then a human comes over to interrupt me, and Persephone's expression changes. At his whispered words, she throws me an annoyed glance and leaves.

Ileana steps in my path before I can follow. "Is this really worth all the trouble?"

"Yes."

"She does not seem to think that way…"

"And she'll end up dead."

Ileana tilts her head, observing me a little too closely. "You like this one."

"Maybe."

After another deep assessment, she moves out of my way and trails behind me.

I don't know what I expected. Persephone has made it clear she doesn't need help, but a goddess living among humans? There must be more to this story.

When I finally find her again, it's in a human house. She's helping a child drink from a bowl while the parents look on. He can't be older than four, with dark curls plastered to his head by sweat. His skin glints in the dim light, probably due to fever.

And still, in Persephone's arms, he's the picture of innocence. His tiny mouth opens and closes around the wooden spoon as she feeds him something—herbs? Seeing her like this only confirms everything I've already observed. She isn't just a goddess, but a truly, deeply *good* one.

I keep out of sight in the entryway, enough that she doesn't notice me. Then the parents' worry assails me.

What if she can't heal him? Since he's been born, it's been one thing after another. I know she has helped humans before…

I glance at the mother, her drawn traits, then at the father. His expression is equally filled with concern.

Persephone has to help. They say she is immune to disease, that the earth itself protects her. And since she has arrived, our crops have never been better, our livelihood easier. Her herbal remedies are the stuff of witches, but she is not. Something, anything—she has to succeed.

I'm so engrossed in their thoughts, in the vision they paint of Persephone, that everything else falls out of focus. Persephone's gaze collides with mine suddenly and flashes light-ning. She hands the bowl of remedy to the mother, then rushes to me, dragging me out.

Within moments she has me out of the house, around a corner, and glares at me.

"Is he yours?" I blurt out. It wouldn't be the first time a deity has given birth through humans, after all.

Persephone gapes at me, her anger morph-ing into outrage. "No!"

"Then why do you insist on staying behind?"

"Because these humans need me."

"To, what? Make potions and crop grow? You're more than that, Persephone."

She scowls at me. "What do you care?"

"I—"

"These people *need me*," she repeats. "Olympus does not."

My focus intensifies on her. On the fire in her words, in her glare, in her very being. "What am I missing here?"

"Nothing. It's none of your concern."

I draw closer. "And if I make it mine?"

Her gaze cools on me. "Then that will make you no better than your brother, will it?"

Stunned into silence, I have no choice but

to watch her leave, presumably toward the house again. A moment later, Ileana emerges from the shadows and touches my shoulder to draw my attention.

"We should leave."

I shake my head, still staring at the spot Persephone last stood on. I've been called many things, but never actually compared to Zeus. I'm definitely not liking it.

As I let Ileana drag me away, something else dawns on me. "You said in immortal school, they teach you things. About us, and so on."

"Hmm."

"What were you taught about Persephone?"

Ileana glances at me, then looks away again. It prompts me to stop, forcing her to face me.

"Tell me."

She sighs, taps her foot, avoiding my gaze still. I wait as patiently as I can, until she finally relents. "Your Fates are involved."

I frown. "I would have guessed as much, given we keep running into each other and I can't stop dreaming of her."

Ileana lets out an exasperated breath.

"No, not those fates. *Your* Fates, Hades. As in, the three sorceresses of Olympus who intertwine the webs of life."

"The what?" What the hell is she going on about?

She stares me, then her expression changes from exasperation to shock and finally to fear. "How do you not know about the Fates?" *How is it... We were not... I need to ask Făt. What is this? What else has been hidden from him?*

"Ileana." I take a step closer. "Tell me. Everything."

Eyes wide, she speaks. And they are words I cannot unhear.

After Ileana's little revelation, I find myself unable to move. My mind is in a whirlwind, trying to determine what, if anything, of her words is truth. But what reason would she have to lie?

I seek my immortal guard out. Her glow radiates not that far off from where I'm sitting on a boulder, ruminating over what I've learned.

And as if by perfect coincidence, Persephone choses that moment to walk past, presumably being done with the little boy now. One look at me, and she rolls her eyes, then starts walking away.

"I'm not here for you," I say without moving.

She stops in her tracks, then whirls on me, hand on her hip. Yet another flare of indignation crosses her expression, and I'm beginning to wonder if I'll see anything else from her anytime soon.

"And you expect me to believe that?"

"No."

The shortness of my answer seems to draw her in, almost despite herself. At first it's one step, then another, and soon enough she's within arm's reach. It's what I've been wanting, what I've been trying to get her to do for the last few days. Yet now that it's here, my mind is anywhere but on what could be.

Instead, it's something completely at odds that blurts past my lips. "Do you know of the Fates?"

She frowns, tilting her head to the side. And yet she says nothing.

"Do you?" I press.

"What, exactly, do you mean by the Fates? As in, the fate of humans, our fate, or…"

"I mean the three sorceresses who run us like pieces on a chess game and fuck with our lives. And the mortals. But most especially, ours." My voice rises, and I stand off the boulder, unable to sit still as Ileana's words echo in my mind. "*Those* Fates."

We stare at each other for a long moment until she finally concedes with a small nod. "Yes, I know exactly what you mean."

"How?"

Annoyance flares on her features again. "What do you mean, how? It's knowledge we all have, no?"

"Not me! I've only just learned of their existence through my immortal guard."

A flicker of indecision replaces her annoyance. "But…"

"Do you actually know someone who possesses this knowledge, too? That there are creatures out there more powerful than us?"

"Yes, I mean I assume everyone in the conclave would know…"

Which means Zeus. He knows, he's known

all along that they exist. Worse, he's also known I had a mate out there, a person whose fate was intertwined with mine, and he hid it from me.

"How did you find out, Persephone? Please. I need to know."

"When my powers didn't work the way they were supposed to, my mother took me to see the Fates. As part of the conclave, she had full access to, well, everything. She swore me to secrecy. I thought it was conclave business." She pauses, searching my features for an answer that eludes me. "You really didn't know of their existence? Your brother never said anything?"

"No, he didn't."

It's my turn to walk away for once, unable to see her and also try to process this information. Unexpectedly, Persephone follows me. I can't say how I know it, other than I feel her presence trailing me.

"What, exactly, did your immortal guard tell you about them? And why did she?"

"Because I was asking her about you, trying to learn the small tidbits you refuse to give me."

A heavy sigh behind me has me turning around.

"Hades, you have to stop this obsession."

"I would. If you were able to look me in the eye, right now, and tell me Ileana was wrong."

"Wrong about what?"

"Telling me our fates are intertwined. That it was decided by the Fates themselves."

Her lips part as she stares at me in shock, but no words escape her. Not of denial, nor of acceptance.

"I thought as much."

Ileana moves out of the shadows then and dutifully opens a portal, without me even having to ask her to. But even as I follow her, back to Olympus and to my lonely chambers, I know this is far from over.

CHAPTER TEN

I wish I could say the next thing I do is storm through Olympus until I run into Demeter, Zeus, and the lot of them and demand some answers. But there's no point for such a confrontation, when the answer to why they hid this from me is staring me in the face. I'm the black sheep of Olympus, the disgrace of this pantheon, and the last thing they'd want is my happiness.

So instead of seeking them out, I go back to old habits and a decanter of ambrosia until I pass out.

When Ileana wakes me up, much later, my anger has abated. It's not Persephone's fault, but it is the conclave's. What else have they kept from us? And how many deities are affected by the Fates' games? Could Hera and Zeus' match also be part of that?

"It is a mess," Frumos says, staring at me as if expecting me to grow three heads. "But sometimes, things are kept from us for our own good."

I jab my finger vaguely in the direction of his voice, since my vision is still too blurry. "No one asked you. Either of you. I could've happily gone on not knowing any of this shit."

Somewhere in the room, Ileana sighs.

"Why did you wake me, exactly?" I ask.

"You said to watch over your girl," Frumos says.

"Not my girl." *Yet.*

He clears his throat. "Regardless, you may want to head into the mortal realm once more."

"And, why?"

"Because a young boy—the one she'd been with—is about to die."

I rub at my face and get up unsteadily, running a hand over my body to cleanse myself. Then I glance into the mirror he's angling toward me. It shows me a boy, the one Persephone had been feeding a remedy to, now in the midst of the woods, heading toward a pit of snakes.

"What the—?"

I materialize there before either of them can stop me. The woods are quiet, meaning that little boy is without his family. How the hell would he have landed here?

I save the questions for later and rush into the bushes, trying to find a trace of his beige tunic. By the time I reach him, he's got barely a foot between him and a snake, talking in gibberish and reaching out for the dangerous predator.

"Erm, kid?"

The boy doesn't react, instead inching closer.

I tiptoe behind him, my attention on the snake, getting ready to blast it away. The boy gets distracted with a twig, and in that moment the reptile lunges. I snatch the human up and incinerate the thing with my free hand.

It's been a while since I've used my deity powers to defend someone. But not so long that I've forgotten they leave a trace in the world of humans. And despite the snake being nothing more than ashes now, there's an odd smoke around it. A very *divine* type of smoke.

Doesn't Hera love using reptiles to do her bidding?

I shake the thought away and place the kid back on the grass, far away from the incident spot. "That was dangerous."

"Lizard, lizard!" the boy cries.

I hold back from rolling my eyes and instead crouch at his level. "It's not a lizard, kid. That was a snake. They—" How do I even mention these things kill?

"—are extremely dangerous," someone finishes behind me.

Persephone. And here we go again.

I glance over my shoulder, watching her approach. Whether because I'm with a kid or have saved his life, her features are less wary than normal.

She holds out her hand when she's close enough. "Come here, Heracles. Your parents were looking for you."

The boy stands on wobbly feet and heads to her, then turns to me and holds his free hand. I wait for Persephone's reaction. When all I get is a small, encouraging smile, I stand and grab his hand, then follow them back into the village.

After we've handed the kid back to his parents, Persephone walks with me some more. She hasn't yet yelled at me to leave, so I'm planning to stick around. At least, as much as she'll allow me to.

She comes to a stop, an odd expression on her features.

"Are you trying to figure out how to politely tell me to fuck off again?"

She sighs, rubs her nape. "Why do you take such interest in me? Is it because you feel you owe me?"

"I... No, it isn't that."

"Then why? Answer me this question, and I'll be honest with you in return."

It's the truth or nothing, Hades. So she didn't really leave me alone, my watcher, she's just out of sight but still within hearing.

Ileana's right, though. If I ever want Persephone to trust me, to really trust me, this is the time.

"Because I dream of you, all right? I've *been* dreaming of you. I didn't know it was you, only these last few weeks, but I've heard your laughter and felt your scent, and— Why are you looking at me this way?"

"Those dreams? You're not alone in having them."

A faint blush colors her cheeks. It takes me a moment longer to realize the meaning of her words. "You mean you've been...about me, too?"

She nods, withdrawing her gaze from mine.

I don't know what to say. Maybe I wasn't wrong in my original assumptions, then, in thinking there's more to this, to us, than simply passengers of an eternal existence. Of course, now that I know we were fated together, it all makes sense.

"Since when?" I finally ask.

"The night of the party."

I think back to when I'd seen her on Earth. "Only a week ago, then?"

The blush deepens. "Not that party."

My eyes widen. "You mean to tell me you've been dreaming of me since Zeus' party, centuries ago?"

She nods, allowing the curtain of her hair

to cover her features. I can't stay away anymore, then. I move closer, kneeling in front of her, and tilt her chin up to better see everything those eyes are trying to hide.

"Persephone… Why not tell me?"

She laughs, a mirthless sound. "You're brother to Zeus. The dreams were most probably another effect of the Fates messing about with us. Plus, everyone knows you're out of my league, as my mother was keen to remind me. Multiple times."

"Your mother is a fool." I run my thumb over her bottom lip, then drop my hand. "It's you who are out of my league."

"You don't have to sweet talk me, Hades. But, I do owe you an answer. And this is it— I never belonged in Olympus. And I thought you didn't, either. It's what attracted me to you in the first place, until that night."

The night I behaved like an oaf.

"And then?"

She shrugs and stands, dusting herself off. "I chose to spend more time on Earth. Found my spot here. I help humans. I'm *good* at helping them, with herbs and plants for their ailments. Though my magic's nothing in Olympus, here, it's enough. *I* am enough."

My heart hurts at her words.

"Don't blame yourself," she says softly. "You couldn't have known, even then. And you were rather drunk when you asked me to entertain."

"I was..." How can I tell her that I was probably so out of my mind with ambrosia, she was the victim of my stupidity?

"That night, though... It was the last straw that made the choice for me. You were so callous, so dismissive when I pleaded to let it go. My mother was silent, and Zeus encouraged you."

I remember that. If I close my eyes, the echoes of his thoughts are still in my mind. *For once, he's acting like my brother.* And I vaguely remember more. That Persephone had stuttered, trying to bloom the flower, and I'd stumbled away from the table. Indifferent to the chaos I had caused.

"When all those deities laughed," Persephone says, "and jeered, and made jokes about me falling short of the Olympian standards... I didn't belong before that party, and I haven't since. Nowadays, I avoid

Olympus like the plague, unless my mother commands me there."

"Persephone, I'm sorry. For all of that. I know better than most how cruel they can be. I've been there."

"I thought you had." She smiles sadly. "I thought you, of all people, would've understood. But when I realized you weren't who I'd thought either...." She shrugs. "Since then, I've been happy. In a place I truly belong. A place where I'm loved, flaws and all. So, I can't go to Olympus. Not with you, not ever."

Before she can leave me again, I step closer, sending us both hurtling into the nook of the house.

"You do belong with me, though. But that is a conversation for another day, and my presence here isn't just about that. I will apologize and find a way to beg your forgiveness, but this, me here, is about much more. Your entire existence is at risk, Persephone."

"Not here. The only thing that's putting me at risk is you."

I can't resist any further then. I've tried, as the gods are my witness I have fucking tried not to be a callous jerk, but I can't any more. The last of my restraint slips away, and I lower my head to hers, allowing our noses to touch, and hold. She kissed me last time, I didn't dream that. But I'll be damned to the depths of Tartarus if I don't taste her one more time, for real.

When our mouths touch, it's a fusion of the senses, a catalyst to my aching body. She melts under my hands, her body soft and pliant, her mouth opening and letting me savor her. Like two pieces coming together, there's no hesitation, no second-guessing. We just...are.

Head tilted back, she lets me explore, even as her hands roam over my back, on my shoulders, and settle at the back of my neck, into my hair. Shivers of delight run up my spine, and I break the kiss.

"You're mistaken. If anyone's putting someone at risk, it's you, my beautiful goddess."

"I'm not the one you deserve."

"You're the one I *need*, Persephone."

She looks up at me, waiting, on the cusp—and then I do the unthinkable. I finally open my heart to her, like she has with me.

"You were never mistaken," I repeat. "Earlier. When you thought we were the same. That I'm different, too. We're both outcasts of Olympus."

She frowns. "How?"

"Because I don't think the Fates were wrong, if they are behind our dreams and interactions. If they fated us together, it explains it all. But only because we were already two sides of the same coin. This draw I feel to you... I, like you, have a defect. Something Olympus sees as a weakness, but that is my strength instead. At least, I hope it is."

"And what's that?"

I take a deep breath, half prayer, half encouragement, then blurt it out. "I hear thoughts. Of gods and goddesses. Zeus has told me since I was young that I'm not man enough, that I'm broken, that I'm unwell."

"You..." She stares at me, trying to understand my revelation. "And mine? You can hear mine, too?"

"No, not yours. It's what jarred me out of my pitiful existence into your orbit. And the more I've seen you, watched you, the more I understand now." I touch her cheek. "Deities are meant to be perfect. You and I, we aren't. Your differences quiet mine, like pieces of the same whole coming together. Perhaps that's yet another reason we're fated."

Her eyes shine with unshed tears. "Hades…"

"You were right, long ago. Let me prove it to you again. Come with me. Please."

She stares at me, her eyes glazed, and then she rises on tiptoes again. Her mouth clashes against mine, less soft and more impatient, demanding. I let her have her fun, trying to wrap my mind around the fact she's not hating me. That she hasn't, ever. Instead, she's simply been waiting for me. As I have for her. Except neither of us knew it.

When she pulls away, I feel the distance in every fiber of my being. It takes all my strength to allow the space she puts between us.

"Not tonight. Hades, I have a responsibility here, a…desire to help. So I can't come, not tonight. But soon."

She kisses me once more, and then leaves me behind, resting my head against the cool brick of the house.

Ileana steps out of the shadows of the nearby house, a smile on her lips. "It worked out well, then?"

"As well as it could."

I've gotten through to Persephone, which is the most important. And while she knows about my darkest secret, something tells me she won't be telling anyone else.

The only question left is, what's *her* darkness?

CHAPTER ELEVEN

I've been back in Olympus for a few days, but I left my thoughts and heart somewhere on Earth with Persephone. It's odd, to think how we've missed each other until now. To realize, truly, that her silent mind is what mine needs.

Lost in thought, I don't hear anyone come in, not until…

For fuck's sake. The thought makes me jump first, then I turn around. Frumos and Ileana share an odd look, half concern, half fear.

"What is it?"

"The Council reconvened again," Frumos says.

I'd been distracted with Persephone, and

this went out of my head. Has it already been a fortnight?

"Why? Did they find something?"

"Of a sort."

With no other information, I follow them into the atrium. Their sour moods are warning I won't like what I see. And, sure enough, the atrium is as packed as last time.

The uneasiness hits me first, followed by the thoughts.

Could have been avoided…

No damned protection…

What we have isn't indestructible…

Should have done more…

They should have trusted us!

I catch sight of Pegasus near a column behind Zeus and walk over to him. "What's going on this time?"

He frowns, running his gaze up and down me. "Where have you been?"

"Out and about."

He rolls his eyes. "Good of you to finally clue in. I think you've picked the worst possible time to fall in love, my friend."

"I haven't—"

"They think they've found Fenrir's immortal guardians," he speaks over me, dismissing my useless denials. "Dead."

My body freezes, and I glance over to the immortals behind me. No wonder they've been struggling to figure out how they felt. Yes, they were created to protect us, but from what they've told me, they've undergone training together. Hearing of their classmates dying can't be easy.

"Where?" I ask Pegasus.

"Near one of the Norse gods' realms."

This doesn't bode well, at all. Either Fenrir killed them, which will mean chaos all over again, or they were killed by outside forces, meaning we're all in danger now.

Zeus catches my eye in the front but says nothing. It takes all my willpower not to march up to him and ask why he hid the truth from me, regarding Persephone. But that would only give him more power, seeing me so unhinged.

No, when I talk to him, it'll be on my own terms, and in a way that, for once, doesn't reflect bad on me.

I look away from him and instead focus on the proceedings. As he did last time, Zeus calls the room to order and wastes no time giving the floor to Odin.

"Your update, mighty Odin."

The old god stands, straight as can be, and levels his good eye on every deity present in the circle, until it finally lands on Zeus. His thoughts are a mess.

I must protect is the only thing I can catch before he speaks.

"As tasked by this Council, we searched far and wide for our comrade Fenrir. While we have not found him, and thus cannot substantiate claims that he attacked one of your own gods, we did make another discovery."

He pauses, his thoughts going haywire. Once I focus on him and only him, I catch the gist of it. He was close to Fenrir. Despite all the claims to the contrary, he saw something in the wolf god and none of this sits well with him. For the head of a pantheon, this is... *Interesting.*

Odin catches himself and continues, "We found his immortal guardians, the two tasked to protect him. Dead. Their throats were slashed by a blade that seemingly has no issues affecting a supernatural."

A voice yells from the crowd, "We should have stuck with the zmei!"

"Aye, those dragon shifters at least looked impressive."

I scowl at the naysayers and move into the middle. They shut up, if only because they want to see what new spectacle I'm about to make of myself.

"We set aside the zmei because they couldn't be trusted to remain objective. I, for one, have had only good service from my immortals."

Silence, then, "I bet you have!"

I glare at the crowd, trying to find the voice. "Come say that to my face."

"Enough!" Zeus growls behind me. "My brother is right, and we are well protected. However… This news is disturbing, and we shall treat it as such. We will stay within our confines in Olympus, and each pantheon should do the same."

I stare at Zeus in shock. Yes, he has now been proclaimed ruler of Olympus, but if I'm hearing his thoughts right, this won't stop here. He intends to do a full lockdown, to stop any god from crossing into any other realm, making us prisoners of our own spaces.

As heads nod all around, Odin's dark-haired son mutters behind his father, "Or, you could tell everyone what is causing this."

"Silence!" Odin says, but it's too late.

Murmurs are rising, whispers continue, and before long the crowd of gods of all pantheons demand to be told. Zeus glares at me as if I'm the sole source of the problem.

Of course, he'd still hold a grudge since last time.

Morrigan takes the stand, surveying us all with her cool eyes. "Odin is not the only one who hunted far and wide, who searched for an answer to this. We have, as well."

One of the Egyptian gods tilts his massive jackal head. "Ah, going off on your own. How unsurprising."

Morrigan narrows her eyes on him. "You know as well as we do, Anubis, that gods don't infight."

Anubis... Ah. He leads the lost souls to their afterlife for the Egyptian pantheon. And he's a dick overall, at least in so far as my encounters with him have led me to believe. Judgemental to a fault, this one.

Morrigan turns her gaze to the rest of them. "You all know about the evils we have each fought. Some, we were able to eradicate, and others, we could only imprison within our own pantheons. It is our belief that the balance has shifted, perhaps because we have been so long removed from the human world. Whatever it is, evil is rising once more and demanding our full attention." A pause, then, "This means we work together. We check on our prisoners. We reinforce our prisons. Whatever it is, we must do it—because if one evil escapes, the rest are sure to follow."

"And what happens if our prisons cannot hold them anymore?" Loki asks.

Ileana *was* right. She read something in this god, something that's already rubbing me the wrong way.

"Then we find another one," Morrigan says. "A stronger one."

I've heard enough. Motioning for Ileana and Frumos to follow me, I head back to my chambers. Pegasus is on my heels, frowning at my sudden mood change.

"What's going on with you?"

"I've been with her—Persephone."

A blank expression, then, "And?"

"And, she and I were meant to be."

"For you to go from one end of the spectrum to the other…"

I shake my head. "You don't understand. No one would. We're… I can't leave her on Earth, and she hasn't taken me seriously. Whatever this is, it's clearly going after deities that are separated from the pack. And I've traveled there enough times to leave a trace, meaning even if she hasn't been on anyone's radar, she is now."

"But she's not—"

I scowl at him. "She's powerful in her own right. And she needs to return here, before Zeus goes into full lockdown."

Pegasus stares at me a moment longer, then nods and claps my shoulder. "Then I will come with you."

"You don't have to."

"What are friends for?"

I nod and turn to my guards, waiting for their safe portal.

I know the minute we get out of the portal that something's wrong. It's too damn quiet, as if the village is holding its breath. I pull out a sword from thin air, and Ileana and Frumos do the same. Pegasus stares between us, before following suit.

"Are you sure about this?" he asks me. He's not a fighter, not by a long shot. But he has been trained, and not that long ago, he was my sparring partner.

"Yes."

Already, I'm straining my ears, trying to capture thoughts—for once actually seeking them out. I need to know where Persephone is. Heart seemingly in my throat, I advance as swiftly as I can. But still there are no thoughts, and the area is unbearably quiet.

Finally, I catch a faint feeling from her — of her essence—and barrel through the rest of the village, uncaring of my surroundings.

"Hades, wait!" Ileana's hiss is inconsequential.

The path leads me in front of a dilapidated house. I dive inside, eyes attempting to adjust to the dark. Then Persephone's there, grasping my hand, and oddly calm.

"You came back."

"I said I would." I inspect the area for trouble, not finding any. She's alone. "What happened, Persephone?"

"The village was attacked in the middle of the night. Everyone fled…"

"And you?"

She looks away. "I couldn't leave this house. When I tried, I was stuck. The barrier, whatever was keeping me here, only dropped recently. I told the humans to leave without me, that I would find them after. They were too scared to not listen."

"You should've come with me when you had the chance."

"The time for *I told you so* is later."

"Yes, I agree." I glance around, only then understanding the other part she told me. "Did you say… You couldn't leave? But that the barrier dropped a few moments ago?"

"Yes, why?"

Whatever was holding her captive here must have realized we arrived. Panic spreads through me, driven up the wall at Ileana's and Frumos' thoughts.

Ambush!

Need to get Hades before —

"We need to leave. Now!"

I grasp her hand in mine and drag her out.

No sooner do we exit the house than it erupts into flames. I still can't see who's attacking us—and then I look up. Bursts of light and darkness hurtle in the sky, like storm clouds. But it's not nature, rather, something worse. Winged creatures, a cross between horses and reptiles, with riders in black helmets. Their heads are the shape of a horse, but with scales. Their riders are hidden under the helmets, but their hands are equally scaled. They hold spears, and it's the energy they charge them with that lights the sky in such obscure hues.

"What is this?"

Persephone whimpers by my side, trying to pull her hand away from me.

"I've got you." I cup her cheeks, focusing her gaze on me. "I won't let anything happen to you."

She opens her mouth as if to say something, but Ileana yells across the pathway.

"We need to leave!"

Another ball of fire hurls itself between us, and Persephone steps back with a yelp. I stumble into Ileana. She grabs my shirt collar and yanks me to her, intending to throw me through the portal she opened in the distance.

This is what I trained for. I cannot let him get hurt right now. No matter what happens with Făt… He has to take care of himself. Hades is my priority.

I tear out of my immortal's grasp, deaf to her cries. I'm going after the woman I'm meant to be with. I have spent the last eons asleep, unaware of all that I could be. Now, I have a chance to prove myself, and I will be damned if I do not.

But as I head toward Persephone, the sky winged creatures descend on us. One in front of her, two more around Pegasus and Frumos. The sound of shouts and clashes of metal fill the air, and I trust them to have my back.

I run toward Persephone, my sword raised high, slashing at the creature. But it moves backward before I can hurt it, its wide eyes on something to the side. I turn, and my stomach drops. *This* is the darkness I'd felt in Persephone.

It permeates her entire being, as if her deity

powers have decided to manifest such. The ground underneath her burns, turning ashy, devoid of life and unable to give life. Houses crumble in the vicinity, as if corroded. Air itself—

"Persephone—"

What is she doing! Ileana yells. Out loud, she says, "Hades, stop her! She'll kill us all!"

I run to Persephone, tackling her and falling to the ground with her. A ball of fire lands over our heads, and I roll us out of the way, then shove her in the direction of a house as I follow. Temporary shelter, at best, but it'll do.

She curls up by the brick wall. Tears are bathing her cheeks, sobs racking her chest.

"Persephone—"

"This is what I meant!" she cries, her eyes wild. "I can't... I'm not who I'm meant to be. I'm a fraud. A nothing. I don't deserve to be in Olympus, let alone with you. This..."

I crush my mouth to hers, stifling her words.

"I don't care. Do you hear me? There's nothing wrong with you. *Nothing.*"

She stares at me as if unable to believe my words.

They're not lies, though. It only makes

sense that if she had repressed her powers, for whatever reason, that doing so would lead to this odd manifestation. Doesn't mean it's irreversible. And even if it is, I don't care.

Shouts from around the house distract me. I don't want to leave Persephone, but I need to make sure everyone else is fine. "Stay here. I'll be back in a moment." There will be plenty of time to deal with this new…development.

I rush around the corner and come face to face with one of the winged creatures…and find myself frozen. Its spear nearly collides with my chest, only to be deflected by a burst of bright light. The rider shades its eyes and forces the creature to retreat.

A moment later, Ileana appears, panting. "Are you unharmed?"

"Yes, thank you. Your magic saved me, I was…" I shake my head. "I don't know what happened, really."

She nods, glancing around in a panic. "We need to leave. There are too many of them, as if they knew we were coming."

It's true. I thought there were a few dozen, but instead we're being faced with more than that. Clashes of swords from a distance draw our attention, as does a groan of pain. Frumos, trying to protect Pegasus. He must've taken the brunt of the hit, as he falls to his knees, his sword above his head.

Ileana takes a step toward him then stops herself. She stares between us, conflict in her expression.

"*GO!* Get him, I'll take Persephone."

She leaves then, released from her duty, and I rush to Persephone once more. Pulling her in my arms, making sure my body protects her, I get us moving again. Balls of fire fall everywhere around us, but still, we make our way as we would in an obstacle course.

Ileana and Frumos rush to us, but it's only as they open the portal that I realize someone is missing.

Pegasus.

I look over their shoulders—to his unmoving form.

"*No!*"

My roar of pain only attracts more creatures. Ileana tries to hold me back, but it takes both their strength to toss me and Persephone into the portal—without my friend, who never should have paid the price of my stupidity.

We enter my chambers like the proverbial marching parade of a funeral. Ileana and Frumos go out on the balcony, their voices low, leaving me with Persephone.

She's been silent since the village, lost in her own thoughts. Under the shock of the attack, and me being right, I assume. Maybe also under the shock of seeing one of our own dead.

We are bred to believe we are immortal. All of us.

And yet, we are not.

Numb, I drop onto the couch, burying my head in my hands. Persephone's there the moment after, holding on to my shoulders, allowing me to sink my face in her lap. She strokes my hair, and the feel of her fingers running through it is the ultimate catalyst. I finally allow the well of emotions to build up, and tears fall, one after another.

Gods never cry.

Gods are never weak.

We are the epitome of what is untouchable, invulnerable, immortal.

Yet here I am, bawling like a baby, and unable to stop.

CHAPTER TWELVE

"Hades."

I jump to, hoping it was all a nightmare. I'd been half dozing off on Persephone's lap, trying to avoid numbing my pain in ambrosia. Ileana and Frumos are still debating on what, exactly, attacked us, when Zeus barges into my chambers. And judging by his thundering expression, the day's events are not, in fact, a nightmare. They're only too real.

"Follow me to the atrium." He glances at my guardians. "Only you, and Persephone. Her mother wishes to see her."

Persephone winces but stands first. I admire her ability to be so collected. All I want to do is sink into the floor and forget about my existence. My one ally here, in Olympus, is now dead, never to be seen again. All because of me.

But Persephone won't let me be weak. She intertwines our fingers and moves, and it's the only thing that keeps me from crumbling. The fact I know she understands. I may not hear her thoughts, but I focus on that silence, drive all my attention toward it, and ignore everything else. Especially Zeus' internal monologue.

By the time we enter the atrium, Demeter is there. I don't focus on the other gods, only on her. Her pinched, yet perfect expression, eyes narrowed on Persephone's hand in mine. Dark hair, same as Persephone's, cascades over a shoulder, pulled in a half-braid. Curly tendrils surround a square face, with thin lips currently pursed. Her icy blue gaze finally lands on me.

She is impressive, Demeter. And clearly, her own inspection of me leaves me lacking.

Demeter sits on a throne, similar to Zeus, as she is one of the oldest conclave members for Olympus. Now that Zeus is supreme ruler, their input will only be required if the realm is in danger. Such as now.

When Persephone sees her mother, she immediately stands straighter.

"Come here, child. It has been long since I laid eyes on you." Demeter's voice is barely above a whisper, but there is still firmness in it. An order.

Persephone doesn't want to let me go, but I gently disentangle our fingers. There is no reason she should endure the punishment I am about to. Before she leaves, I tug her into my arms one more time. Ignoring everyone else, I lower my head and kiss her, lingering as long as I'm allowed.

"That is quite enough," Demeter says. *Of all the gods to lay her eyes on, it had to be the most despicable of Olympians. No matter. Some time away, and it'll cleanse her mind of him.*

Persephone goes to her then, but all hesitation has left her steps. And her strength gives *me* the strength needed to ignore Demeter's mental bitching.

"Hades," Zeus says, drawing my attention to him. "You're in trouble this time."

That, if nothing else, surprises me. And jars my focus to my current standing. I have no allies here. Not even my guards. And though Persephone is on my side, I don't want her to create issues for her. I'd meant for her to return to Olympus quietly, not… Fated or not, she deserves a peaceful existence after the mess I've already caused in hers.

She takes a step closer, opening her mouth, but Demeter clenches her hand and tugs her to her side, whispering furiously to her.

Is that what this is, then? Zeus, my dear brother, unable to find a cause or a solution to a mess of his own making—there's no doubt he's involved in this, to some extent—and thus turning to me. The perfect scapegoat.

I clear my throat. "In trouble for what, exactly? All I did was protect Persephone and bring her home."

"And you caused the death of one of our own."

Low blow. The pain hits me, rawer than ever. I avoid staggering, instead clenching my teeth and tilting my chin upward. I won't let Zeus see me crumble.

"It wasn't his fault!" Persephone says. "We were attacked, by winged creatures—"

Demeter scoffs. "Winged creatures? What is this nonsense?"

I meet Persephone's gaze, ignoring her mother. And I shake my head, once. Her expression falters. I wish there was a way to convey what's in my heart, but there isn't. I can only hope I won't drag her down with me.

"Do you not even feel remorse?" Zeus asks. *You should. It will take me millennia to clean up the mess you've left behind!*

A shard of ice lodges itself in my chest. "Don't talk to me about remorse! You—*liar!*" I march toward him, jabbing a finger in his face. "All this time, playing the perfect would-be ruler. All this time, pretending to be honest, accusing others of lying. When through it all, you've been the worst of them."

Zeus glances around, then back at me. He smirks. "I don't know what you mean."

"Yes, you do. Because you've known my entire life I'm fated to be with Persephone, and you hid that from me. Didn't you?"

How did he find out! Demeter's panicked thought almost makes me turn her way, but I don't. My focus is on my brother, and him alone.

Lightning blazes in his eyes, and I prepare to defend myself. But Zeus doesn't strike me. Instead, he stares back at me, unmoved. *It doesn't matter, brother,* he thinks, loud and clear. *Whatever you may have found out, it's useless. Because I now have the perfect way to ensure you'll be out of my way for good, cast somewhere I can't be blamed if anything should happen to you. The oracles can't foresee you dethroning me if you no longer exist. And as for your dear Persephone... Well, she'll find others, I'm sure. After all, gods being fated is a myth, no?*

I clench my fists. Never have I wanted to strike him more than in that moment. He's doing this knowing full well that no one else hears his admission, only me. Forever keeper of this secret.

As his smirk widens, Zeus dismisses me and waves toward Demeter.

She stands, clearing her throat. "Regardless of what harm you think was done to you, you have done much, much worse to Olympus."

"Really?" I cross my arms over my chest. "Do tell me. This should be entertaining."

Why, the insolence— She takes a deep breath and continues in a forced, even tone. "You broke many laws, perhaps the two biggest being that you killed one of our own, and showed yourself to humans."

"There were no humans around!"

"A little boy saw you."

Of course. With my luck, it shouldn't be surprising.

Already, I knew the moment I entered the atrium that it would not be a good ending for me. It's time I accept it, and with a bit of luck it'll lead to somewhere with a good beginning. After all, if nothing else, this entire mess has made it clear I don't belong in Olympus. Never have, never will.

"You're aware of our dilemma," Zeus continues. "After the pantheons undertook the check-ups we requested, it has become apparent some evils have, indeed, escaped. The Valkyries of the Norse have offered to hunt them down for the rest of us. In the meantime, we need a spot to imprison them all next, and to transfer them. Somewhere they can never pose a risk."

Of course. Let everyone else do the work.

"And I presume you identified a location already?"

"Yes. Tartarus."

I start at the name. I know of it, of course, we all do. It's a barren land, a realm of darkness and shadows where human souls wander, unseen and ignored, since we retired from the world.

And its mention… Now, it all makes sense.

"You wish me to become the new jailer, then?"

"No!" Persephone cries, unable to help herself. "Mother, you can't do this. Hades was protecting me!"

Sure he was. "Hush, child."

Persephone ignores her, instead taking a step toward me. "And you know! Mother, you *know* we're fated together! By the Fates themselves!"

Demeter's tone is harsh as she yanks her back. "Enough of this." To me, she says, "Yes. To answer your question, you are to take over this domain, and do as you please with it."

"What of the souls down there?"

"Exile them, banish them, keep them," Zeus says in a bored tone. "I care not. Your purpose there is one, and one alone. To keep that evil contained."

"I will need more help than just me."

"Then you can recruit others."

As if anyone sane would join me in this isolation quest. I see how it is. But I won't give in to their insidious thoughts, nor show the pain this is causing me. Because if anything, it's only causing me one particular agony — that I won't see Persephone for a while.

"Very well," I say, feeling the weight of her teary gaze on me. "When do I begin?"

"Now." Zeus claps his hands and opens a portal, then stands back, ignoring Persephone's gasp. "I trust you can summon whatever you need in there?"

I step toward it, clenching my jaw, trying my darndest not to look at her. "Yes."

"Good. Valkyries offered to escort the various evils, a few at a time. You can expect them to arrive in groups as soon as they catch said evils." Zeus pauses, meeting my gaze arrogantly. "Do try not to screw this up."

A bitter laugh escapes me. "Screw up? In your eyes, I will always be *the* screw-up. But I have gotten used to that, and I expect nothing else." I step closer, dropping my voice to a whisper. "I know what you're doing. And you won't get away with it. Sooner or later, you'll pay for your arrogance." I step back before he can say anything and glance at Persephone one more time. "Until we meet again, beloved."

Because I have to hope this is not the end. At least, not forever.

With a last sigh, I straighten my back and step through the portal.

CHAPTER THIRTEEN

The portal drops me into a realm I should be familiar with, but I'm not entirely. At some point, most of us tried to enter this vast land of nothingness in a way to gain some edge. Our version of rebellion.

Tartarus has existed since the beginning of time itself. It was a story we all grew up with, something we dared ourselves to broach. There was a time our parents blocked all realms from accessing this one…

The last time I'd been here? Zeus had dropped me and left me alone. He'd only learned of my *special* powers, and wasn't about to get through Olympus with having a freak god for himself. So in his youthful mind, dropping me here was the best thing he could do. For himself, that is.

I guess things don't change that much over many eons, after all.

I don't know how long I spent here, assailed by souls and human ghosts, until someone came to get me. It was Pegasus, and that was the beginning of our friendship.

He'd heard us quarreling right before, and when Zeus returned to Olympus without me, Pegasus forced Hermes into tracking down where he'd gone. And so it had led them to Tartarus. And to me. Hermes immediately thought it had been my fault, but Pegasus knew better. And even though prior to that we had barely interacted, he soon became my best friend. A better brother to me than Zeus ever was.

And now, here I am again.

I drop my gaze to the ground, and the full pain of Pegasus' loss rattles through my body. My legs sway and, unable to hold myself up, I kneel, digging my fists in the arid earth. Hot tears pour down my cheeks, and though I try to control my sobs, I cannot.

In all of Olympus and the pantheons, Pegasus was my one true friend. I have passable relations with other deities like Morrigan, but Pegasus was truthful with me. Honest. Always there. And I repaid him with mistrust, disloyalty, and dragging him into a fight that was his end.

Yet I cannot regret it, not fully. If it hadn't been for his help, I couldn't have saved Persephone. We couldn't have all gotten out of there, alive. Was it worth it, to lose my only friend? Especially now that I lost her, too?

I'm under no illusion. No one, least of all a goddess, will enter this exile with me. Because it's nothing short of an exile, at the end of the day. For however long they see it fit, I'll serve my penance here. In this valley of nothing. I will speak with only spirits, and have no connection to the outside, other than through visitors.

Even that will probably be monitored, if I know Zeus. This is his best way of getting me out of the way, that much is apparent. And while I could fight him, what would be the point? I never belonged there. In a way, he and the conclave did me a favor. A chance to start anew, in an area I can devise to my heart's content, and with no rules to follow other than my own.

And if Pegasus' death has taught me anything, it's that I won't let it sit in vain. He was able to be selfless, the way only he could, in his quest to help me and protect me. I won't repay that effort with my indifference. I'll do my duty, I'll protect Olympus. But I won't be miserable. I've played that game once before with myself, and it's time I outgrow it.

If I'm to remain here, I'll make this Underworld my home, and I'll become its Lord.

Easier said than done. After wandering the lands of the place far and wide, I can't settle on where to begin. Everywhere I turn, I'm met with ghosts of human spirits and a vastness of land that's gone unchecked for too long.

Rivers abound, as do mountains in various areas. Where there should be sky, I find only a vast emptiness. How can someone live here and still hold on to light?

I force the dark thoughts away. Evidently, I'll need a home, and perhaps an area to discuss with spirits. If I'm to live here, I'll want a good, solid relationship with them. There might even be things we can help each other with.

And there's the matter of the prison and ensuring it remains a prison no one can escape… I glance around, taking it all in, and not for the first time missing the ambrosia.

Before I can even think about conjuring myself some, a spark of lightning bursts in the distance, followed by another, and another, and something that rolls like thunder. I approach the spot carefully. Surely Zeus wouldn't bother to come here?

It's not him, though. It's a blond god, with a hammer in his right hand. And he's not a stranger, either. I've seen him before, by Odin's side—Thor. And he's surrounded by three women, their long hair in braids, and dressed in a full body of armor.

Upon my arrival, Thor turns to me, settling his gray eyes on me. "Father said we are to bring our captures here. Are you Hades?"

"I am."

He nods, thumping his chest. "Thor." He gestures to the women. "And my Valkyrie guards."

I wait. His thoughts are all over the place, while the Valkyries assess the area. Curious, I peer into their minds—they're identifying weaknesses I hadn't even thought of.

"Where, exactly, are we to bring our evils, once we catch them?" Thor asks in the end.

I point to the farthest peak, filled with a reddish tinge. "Tartarus."

"And what will guarantee they cannot escape?"

I sigh. I'd been wondering the same thing, and I worked out a small solution. "I plan to separate this land and ensure it's kept aside from all others. Tartarus will only remain here, and the rest..." I shrug under the Valkyries' assessing gaze. "I haven't gotten that far yet. But one idea did strike me for the prison. Since the evils of our worlds belong to each of our realms, it would help if gods from each pantheon come here and cast binding enchantments."

Thor frowns. "Like a mixed pot of spells, to keep prisoners in?"

One of the Valkyries says, "Each pantheon

would thus ensure their enchantments would protect not just their own, but other pantheons. One evil from Asgard would not know how to bypass an evil from Olympus."

"Exactly. One of our Titans, for example, could rattle our enchantments, but they won't be able to rattle yours. And if they do, I'll get wind of it and warn anyone of impending doom."

Thor rubs his beard, then checks with the Valkyries. "I approve of the idea. What do you need from us?"

"Add your enchantments to the land and ask a few gods from every pantheon to do the same. For obvious reasons, my reach is limited."

His eyes narrow on me. Perhaps he hasn't yet heard of my exile, or doesn't understand it as such. Whichever the case is, he nods. "I will, and I will send more. Thank you."

The moment after he's gone, as are the Valkyries. One down, only…what, a few dozen left?

I turn back to Tartarus. A faint reddish tinge separates the regular land from the rest. I step backward, and then some, until there is a breadth of space between me and what's soon to become the best prison the world has ever known. Then I hold my hands out in front of me and clench my fists.

The ground responds, rolling and molding to my will. It bucks like a willful horse, splitting and rearing back, becoming that which I envision. A foreign land, a split land…and a river separating me from the rest of it.

On shaky legs, I head back to the mountain I'd been eyeing for my own home. Once there, I raise my hands again.

Time to truly carve out my destiny.

By the time I'm done with the castle that'll be my home, it looks like a half-assed attempt. Not surprising—Poseidon's always been the artistic one, not me.

I've chosen a mountain far away from Tartarus, but within view of all the realm. And little by little, I carved a vision of my own home in it. I've gotten halfway through, and, really, it'll only be me who lives here for now. So half is large enough.

As I stare at my creation, it looks half the mountain was meant to be a work of art, and the rest is, well, a mountain. But, it'll be good for now.

I prepare to head in and carve out the inside, when another portal opens. This time, it's two familiar faces that tumble out—Ileana and Frumos. And, dare I say it, they don't seem to be fighting anymore.

"You two seem to have solved your issues."

Ileana blushes and is quick to change the subject. "We came to help."

I shake my head. "No, not this time. You both have done enough."

"What?" Frumos frowns. "You cannot release us from being your guards. You need us now more than ever!"

I had wondered if they would arrive, and I can only assume the delay is from not being told where I was initially. With a sigh, I gesture to the area.

"Need you here, where only the dead come? I'll be safe, but thank you for the concern," I add wryly. "And I can, indeed, release you. When Zeus banished me here, he practically made me lord of this particular realm. Which means I have the power, now."

I glance at each of them in turn. "I don't deny your help would be invaluable here, but you and I both know more things are happening on the surface than down here. Go, be free of your chains and find your own purpose. Perhaps you'll help others, as you did me. You deserve better than this hellish hole."

They both share a glance, my words taking them by surprise.

This means we are—

—free to do as we wish, Ileana finishes for him.

Their connection warms me. They probably don't even realize how well their thoughts align. The kiss I'd shared with Ileana seems so long ago, as to be almost forgotten. There's no jealous bone in my body as far as they're concerned.

And still, Ileana turns to me and walks closer. She rises on her tiptoes and kisses my cheek. "Thank you. It is an invaluable gift you provided us. But this will not be the last time we see you, Hades."

"Perhaps not. But for now, it is. Be happy, with the one you truly deserve."

She steps back, joining Frumos. Hand intertwined with his, she smiles at me. "Happiness does not have to be a one-time thing, Hades. Persephone waits for you. You only need to ask her to come."

Her words are like shards to my heart. Must she say them, no matter how truthful they are?

Persephone did say Olympus is the last place she wishes to be. But I have to hope things will change now that I'm not around. Perhaps they'll all be focused on my disgrace, and not think of hers.

"I won't do that to her. She should live a good life in Olympus, not be stuck down here." I force a grin. "Besides, I have all the company I need."

"Not yet." Frumos laughs. "But you will, soon enough."

They disappear with those parting words. A moment later, or what seems like a moment later, another portal opens and in come some satyrs. Half-goat, half-men, they are workers in Olympus, used for menial chores, deity errands, and more. I never truly paid them attention, nor have most deities, I'd imagine.

Stunned, I count half a dozen. Their hooved feet create a beat as they walk toward me, then stop. Multiple pairs of chocolate eyes stare at me, as if waiting for instructions.

When I simply stare in dimwitted stupefaction, one of them, with salt-and-pepper hair, speaks to me. "Sire, we are here to help. The immortals let us through."

"Help with...what, exactly?"

"Building your Underworld."

"But... Won't you miss Olympus?"

"We do not belong," says another. "And neither do you. We heard of your exile and wish to join you. Here, we have a chance to be ourselves without being seen as less than."

How many times will I hear these same words, and how many times will they continue to shock me?

"Will you allow us to stay, sire?" asks another, a younger one.

"I..." I stare at their hopeful faces.

Ileana and Frumos let them through... Of course they did. I hardly see an Olympian doing me a favor these days. And if they went against

Zeus like this, how can I refuse? Especially when these poor souls are as suited to this place as I am.

"Of course. Stay as long as you wish and leave whenever you are ready to."

One of them has already turned his attention to the half-finished castle behind me. "How can we help?"

I'm not sure how much time passes. What I know is we work hard, and harder still, and in between, portals open every once in a while, with some deity or another coming to add their enchantments to Tartarus. No evils have yet been brought, not until the prison itself is ready.

One such day, as we finish the carving of the audience hall in my new home—a satyr's idea, as he mentioned souls would be more comfortable in an enclosed space—I get another visitor.

One of my satyrs—I've come to think of them as my friends, really—comes to me.

"An Egyptian is here!"

This should be interesting…

I toss the cloth I'd been using to wipe my face, and step outside. In Olympus, deities may not lift a single finger, but here, I promised to be more than what I was created.

It's night now, and the ceiling above this place is darker than ever. I've been sending bursts of energy into it to keep it lighted, but it will take more than that.

So it's no wonder I don't see my visitor until I almost run into him. Then his jackal ears register. I've always found it odd, how these Egyptians choose to keep their half-animal, half-human forms. *To each their own.*

"I am Anubis," he says. "Come to add my enchantment to Tartarus."

"Thank you. You can find it through there." I point him in the direction, expecting he will follow it without trouble. Most of them have so far.

But he's not done. Instead of leaving, he looks me up and down. "You are the one who will protect us?"

"Yes." I don't mean to sound defensive, but it comes across as that.

A half-snort escapes him. "Then we are in trouble."

Anger flares through me, but I tamp it down. "How about you go do your bit? Then I'd suggest you leave my realm."

With a dark glare my way, he listens and disappears.

Another voice replaces him. "I see you are still not making any friends."

"I-Ileana?" I frown at her. Her mere appearance lights up this entire dump. Has it only been days since I've last seen her, or weeks? "What are you doing here?"

"I come bearing a gift." Her eyes land on the palace, and she smiles. "You did well, you know."

"And you seem happy."

She gives me a secret smile, followed by a faint look of contrition.

"Don't feel like you owe me for your happiness, Ileana. We both know that no matter what spark was there, Frumos is the one for you."

The twinkle in her eyes seems to burn brighter. "The only one."

Her words, though candid, remind me of

my only one. The one outside of this realm, the one I may not see for too many eons to count… If I ever get out of here, that is.

I chuckle. "Now, where's this gift you tease me with?"

She whistles, and out of the darkness comes a little furball. Only, it's…an odd one. I crouch lower, trying to understand what it is I'm seeing. It's only once Ileana shines some light that I realize it's a dog.

He comes up to my knees, but instead of one head, he has three, each one adorned with floppy ears. And…a snake for a tail. His fur is grey mixed with brown, and his eyes are the color of a muddy lake.

One tiny nose comes to sniff my hand, eliciting a chuckle from me. "You've brought me one of Apophos' kids?" The god is a recluse, a monster more than deity, one who has chosen to keep his reptilian form rather than take on a human appearance like the rest of us. Yet another outcast…

Ileana laughs. "Hardly. He was wandering Earth by himself. I could've left him there, to annoy humans in a few years, or…" A shrug. "The choice was simple."

"I can't keep him here, Ileana. It would be inhumane."

"Not if you give him the guidance he needs." She glances from me to him. "Believe me, you are well-suited for each other. Oh, and his name is Cerberus."

She's gone in a flash of light, leaving more than just the puppy behind. Above my head, stars glint in the ceiling above, imploding light onto this dreary world. And, just like that, it's starting to feel more and more like home.

I turn my attention back to the furball, reaching out a hand and scratching behind one ear. While one head likes it, the other tries to bite at me. I gently nudge its muzzle.

"We'll get along just fine, I'd say."

I get up then, and move back to my home. Little by little, this place is becoming...better. It may just be me and the satyrs, and the souls, but already they're coming to me for advice. Soon, all humans who enter here will pass through my gates.

I peer down at the dog. "And maybe you can help out, my newest friend."

When we enter my home, Cerberus bounds around in between the satyrs' hooves, barking as his tiny snake tail tries to reach someone to bite. I can't help another laugh, and it sounds good in this place.

Now if only I could get the one goddess my heart desires, everything would be complete.

CHAPTER FOURTEEN

Time passes differently down here. Or, so it feels. It might just be the lack of ambrosia clouding my mind, or that fact I finally have a purpose. I'm accepted. I belong.

At first, it was hard to use so much deity power—after eons spent drunk out of my mind with ambrosia, it left me exhausted. But little by little, I built up endurance. To the point I'm finally reaching my full potential, the one I shunned time and time again.

With each passing day, I find the satyrs' thoughts less unnerving. They've become background noise, part of the world. But their presence here keeps me grounded, reminding me the work I'm doing is important, and also, my choice.

Cerberus grows like crazy. And since no one's come demanding his return to some other realm, I accepted Ileana's gift whole-heartedly. His consciousness grows all the time, and he's started testing me. Mentally, that is. I find it builds more and more of a connection between us.

And he's not the only one...

The souls have taken a liking to me. I was surprised when the first one came to me, introducing himself as an olden king who'd been in the Underworld for ages. He explained how death worked for them, and how out of sorts all souls feel once they enter the Underworld. How they don't belong, and also feel like they've been thrust into the biggest hell on Earth.

I'd already realized Tartarus would hold the evillest, but the other souls? They had nowhere to go. Other than roam for ages the land. Their thoughts, as I meet each and every one, become the sole driving force behind my next days' work.

There has to be something I can do, some

way I can ensure the souls who don't deserve punishment live out their eternal rest, freely and happily. Not just for my own sanity—there's only so much human complaint I can deal with and not lose my mind—but also for their eternal soul.

Amid all these conversations taking place, and me trying to find a solution, Morrigan comes to visit. She materializes one day in a tornado of dark green smoke and fresh scents, seeking me out the moment she's fully formed.

"Hades."

I step to her and pull her into a hug. She smells like the freshest of meadows after a rain, and I linger a moment longer. Questions are on the tip of my tongue—about Olympus, about the Council, about Odin and Fenrir…and Persephone. But I hold them all back, instead only focusing on one.

"Come to add your enchantments?"

She nods, a twinkle in her eyes. "Among other things."

"Tartarus is through there." I point in the direction, much as I've done with every other deity. "Find me when you're done."

Moments later, she's back, surveying my

castle with interest. "You did all this in just a few weeks of being here?"

I shrug. "I had time on my hands."

"And focus."

"Meaning?"

"Come now, Hades. We both know you have been in a stupor of ambrosia for eons."

There's little I can do to deny it. "True."

"Will you say no to a drink with an old friend, then?" She produces a decanter, and I grin.

"I'd never dream of saying no to you."

I lead her inside my new home, and we open the fresh brew.

"Dionysus' best," she says.

"Thank you." I take a sip, then two. The liquid tastes sweet going down my throat, like a well-acquired taste. Even better than Zeus' reserve... But I'm no longer devoured by my need to consume the entire thing. Instead, I sip it slowly. "So, to what do I owe the pleasure, besides everything?"

Cerberus chooses that moment to step in. *Food. Food. Food!* His incessant, childish thoughts assail me, and I barely hold back a laugh. He's already grown from the puppy stage to what a regular human dog would be like. In a few more days, I'll have to fix him some housing outside.

Morrigan watches as he nudges my knee, expecting more petting. "New friend?"

"Of a sort. Gift from my immortal guard, before she left."

Her jaw drops. "They did not stay?"

"I wouldn't let them. Not when there's much more use for them above ground."

Morrigan twirls her drink. "I suppose. Although, they *were* bred to protect us. No matter, perhaps they can aid in the human realm with all the zmei debacle taking place." When I say nothing, she changes topics. "What Zeus did is unfair. And some Olympians agree, you know."

I shrug. Morrigan only knows of my exile, not the part about me being fated to Persephone and Zeus hiding that from me. Which means there's only so much I can tell her. She's loyal enough she'll fight my battles for me, and that's the last thing I wish. More than most, I'm aware of the duality of Olympians. And being here, far removed from such nonsense, I no longer feel the burden of the life I'd led. Perhaps it's that which makes it easier to speak my mind, for once.

"They can agree all they want, it doesn't mean anything will change. And, in the end, Zeus did me a favor. We both know I don't belong there."

What a horrid way to live. Morrigan's expression falters. "Then where do you belong?"

"Here. You may find it hard to believe, but it's the happiest I've ever been."

"No, I do not find that hard to believe at all." She sighs. *You never did belong, but for a reason, my friend.* "I must warn you, though, putting all these evils in Tartarus... Your idea of all our enchantments was genius."

"But? Let me guess. You think it's not enough."

"I wish it were. But there is much we ignore, and no one has been able to figure out where Fenrir disappeared. And he is not alone..." She takes a deeper swallow of the drink. "I have lost a deity or two, as well."

"Who?"

She shakes her head. "It is not important. Suffice it to say, I no longer believe these incidents are unrelated."

"Yet Zeus didn't care for my explanation.

Those winged creatures weren't an illusion, Morrigan."

"I believe you. All it means is there is a force out there designed to go against us. And while we may round up all the evils we *are* aware of, then what will happen to the ones we are not aware of? The ones lurking in the shadows…"

A delicate shudder runs through her, and I step closer, touching her shoulder lightly. "All we can do is attempt it. When you started talking about this idea, I thought it was crazy. In practice, it's even more so."

"But we both know a time will arrive when it will not be enough."

"And I'll be here to raise the alarm."

She nods, pensive. "When that time is near, you can count on me and mine."

"Thank you."

She glances around once more, then at me. "You are right, you know. I can see the happiness in you." She reaches for my hand, squeezing it before letting go once more. "But before I leave, there is something I must tell you. You did not belong, not because there is something wrong with you, Hades. Simply because Olympus did not deserve you."

Kind words, but we both know the truth. I show her out of the castle, both taking our time, Cerberus on my heels. Once we're on the steps overlooking the land, Morrigan takes it all in. Frowns.

I try to see it as she does. Though it's cleaner than before, and I've raised more riverbeds to separate the areas—especially from Tartarus—it is nonetheless a rather arid land. Souls float around in the distance, their glowing forms providing a little décor.

"Where do your good souls go, Hades?" Morrigan asks.

I blow out a breath. "To be honest, I've been trying to figure that out myself. Tartarus is the land of evil, but I've yet to decide what to do with the pure souls."

She smiles, her eyes glittering with magic. "Care for some help?"

I'd be a fool not to accept. Morrigan is a sorceress among deities, so I follow her to the land I had eyed earlier. "I'd hope the heroes and good souls have somewhere to stay, somewhere peaceful and idyllic."

Morrigan glances around, then touches

the pendant around her neck and mutters some words in old Gaelic. Within moments, rivers stream, grass grows, and flowers blossom. A few more moments pass by, and the earth changes and rolls as it had under my hand. Only, rather than my poor attempts, she makes it...divine.

"Think they will like it?"

I bark out a laughter. "See for yourself."

Some souls have already entered, exploring, laughing like children. To provide this to them, when they suffered so much, fills me with indescribable joy.

Morrigan smiles fondly. "Good. Now you only need a guardian for this realm of yours. Someone to ensure the right souls land in the correct place."

"And soon, I'll find one."

She hugs me again, then leaves. I stand there for long moments, appreciating everything I've accomplished in so little time. Wondering about everything I could have, if I'd gotten off my ass much, much earlier.

In the end, there's no point for such ruminations, especially not around the conflict, what I've lost, and what I could've changed.

Even Persephone. I will wait for her forever if I have to, forever and more to get my chance and return to her. But in the meantime, it can't stop me from living. This, right here, is my focus.

And the fact the souls are happy, which means I'm doing my job right. I may have failed at being an Olympian, but I can't fail at this. Not when there's so much to create, so much to enjoy, and so much to see blossom.

"Sire, we are ready for the next stage."

I snap out of my thoughts and meet the satyr. He looks past me, eyes wide at the new fields for the souls.

"What do you think we give it a name, my friend?"

"I, sire?"

I wait, letting him think it through.

"Elysian," he whispers. "In our language, it translates roughly to *divine*."

I nod. "I like it. From here on out, it'll be known as the Elysian Fields."

With one last glance, I head back to my palace, wondering what Persephone would think of all this. What's she doing in Olympus, or has she gone back to the humans? Would Demeter have allowed her? And most of all…does she even miss me?

Our encounters were too brief to have developed that connection, but oh I do yearn to do it. More than I've ever wanted anything in my entire existence. And it has nothing to do with the Fates playing with our hearts, or our destinies. This need inside me is all me, all fire and lust and a desire to worship her.

Which is probably why, when I see her on the steps to my home, I stop dead in my tracks, not believing my eyes. And then she turns and smiles, and my world fractures all over again.

"Hello, Hades."

I stagger forward one step, then another. Aware only of my heartbeat increasing, the fading environment, and her scent, getting closer. I must be moving toward her, but not consciously. All I know is I'm standing less than a foot away, and she's smiling at me with those glittering violet eyes.

"Persephone." My voice sounds hoarse, like I've gone and swallowed something hard. "What are you doing here?"

Closer still, I catch the slight tremble in her hands before she wrings them together. She bites her lower lip, going for a brave smile, but her words come out just a tad shaky.

"Was hoping you might have room for one more…?"

I frown at her. "One more what?" Has she come to seek a home for some pet or, worse yet, another deity?

The thought threatens to shatter my breath, so I focus on her face instead. Waiting. *Waiting.* She gulps, tightens her hold on her hands, and straightens her back.

"Person. Or, rather, resident."

I take another step toward her. Her scent overpowers me. My body betrays me, yearning for her, yet not daring to hope she's saying what I think she is.

"Who?" I breathe, barely a few inches away from her.

"Me." She glances around. "I know the darkness in me is wrong. I know it's because I haven't trained my powers, but perhaps here I can. And— That's not why, Hades." She finally meets my gaze, tears filling hers. "I told my mother off, and I've about had it with Olympus. It took me this long to come because I was trying to find out more information and see if I could still continue helping out above ground, but it doesn't matt—"

I cut off her ramble the only way I can. With a kiss as searing as the promise it holds, pulling her into my body until I'm the only thing that's keeping her standing, and her legs are shaking, her hands grasping my shirt.

She draws back just enough to stare at me. "I take it you have room, then? For me, here, in your life?"

"My darling, I thought you'd never ask."

Our kiss this time is softer, stronger, consuming… and without thinking twice about it, I whisk us out of the public eye and into my personal chambers.

Persephone steps out of my embrace, taking in our surroundings. "Hades, this is—"

I tug on her hand, hating the distance and finding myself inching closer yet again. "Inconsequential. *You* are my focus now." Without waiting for her retort, I'm kissing her again, cupping her cheeks and allowing myself to feel everything I haven't before.

With one hand, I remove her dress and cast aside my own clothes. And then we're naked, and she's walking backward to my bed, a sultry smile on her lips. "I dare say it's time to make new memories, no?"

I grin. "With pleasure."

When we clash together, the hotness of her skin burns mine, inflaming me even more. Persephone turns at the last moment, pushing me on the bed and straddling me. Inch by inch, she kisses every bit of my skin, until her mouth wraps around me, drawing me in deep.

A hiss escapes me and I tangle my hand in her hair, unsure whether I want to pull her off me or beg her to take me deeper. Persephone makes that decision for me, tightening her hold on me until I explode.

Panting, I wait until she rises above me, licking her lips. Her eyes are shining, amused at my complete lack of control, no doubt. "For someone who can read thoughts, you sure don't do a good job reading mine, beloved."

I flip us over, growling as I hover above her, kissing her neck. "Don't you remember, *beloved*? Yours are the only thoughts I can't hear."

She smiles at my reminder, her eyes shining with recollection, but I'm already moving down her body, tasting every inch of skin I can get my hands on. And I only stop when her sweet honey is on my lips and her cries are echoing in my chamber.

Then, and only then, do I rise back over her. Tease her, my cock at her entrance, prolonging the torture for us both. Until Persephone tosses her head, arches her back, and wraps her legs around me.

"Here's a thought you don't have to guess," she whispers in my ear. "Take me, now, Hades, before I lose my mind."

On a groan, I drop my head to her chest, kissing and nibbling on the skin I can reach, and drive into her. Her hot sheath is all I feel, snug enough that I see stars. And then Persephone moves against me, driving me that bit deeper in, and I let go.

For the first time in my eons of living, nothing else exists except this gorgeous goddess beneath me and the fire we create together.

I wake up to my bed smelling like violets, and

turn over. Persephone's watching me and grins widely. Her hands come to rest on my chest, as if she can't help but draw closer, needing to feel me just as I yearn to.

Never would I have expected to get my own realm, and the goddess I most wanted in it. But to get here? Everything was worth it. Every, little, bit. I would give more and forever to have her with me.

I pull Persephone even tighter, lowering my head to kiss her. The moment after my lips move to her cheek, her nose, her forehead, sprinkling kisses everywhere as she throws her back and giggles.

"Spring personified, in my own bed."

With a thrust of my hips, I've got her straddling me, the only thing keeping us apart the thin sheet between us. Persephone gasps, her eyes darkening as they had last night. I'm reminded of her moans under my fingers, her fevered kisses, and above all, her calling out my name.

"What do you think? Reckon you'll stay awhile?"

She leans closer, allowing her hair to cascade around us. Her eyes sparkle, the corners of her lips tug upward, and she smiles softly. "As long as you'll have me."

"How's eternity, my darling?"

She smiles wider and falls into my embrace. The way I fell into her, so, so long ago.

CHAPTER FIFTEEN

"Are you ready?"

I face Persephone, turning my back to the mirror I'd been pacing in front of. Her long hair cascades down her back in a tumble of curls, pinned with an amethyst comb. Somehow she looks even more in radiant in her silver gown. My heart does a funny thing, halfway between constricting and doing backflips.

"Not nearly," I answer her. "But with you by my side, beloved, I'll face anything."

She chuckles and closes the distance between us, wrapping her arms around my neck and rewarding me with a kiss. "You can do this, I have no doubt." Then she promptly drags me by the arm out of our chambers and down to my very own audience hall.

The *this* she's referring to is my first ever official audience with souls. I've had side conversations over the last weeks, it's impossible not to. Souls are practically everywhere here. And they've sought me out, more and more. In the end, Persephone was clear—it was time to set up something, an open path of communication between them and me.

Which brings me to now. My footsteps falter as we near the audience hall. The large, white ash doors are closed, taunting me. Behind them, I can already catch trickles of thoughts.

This is a mistake, a mistake, I'm not dead! There has to be a way out of here…

I hope he can help me find her, it's been so long I've been without her…

Persephone nudges me, smiling. "You *can* do this, Hades," she repeats. Then she lets me go, knowing I need to do this at my own pace, and opens the door to walk inside.

She's taken to this world with an ease I would not have expected. Her kindness and openness to listen is like honey to these poor souls, who are so desperate for affection after so long living on their own.

I take a deep breath, clenching and un-clenching my fists. This is my realm, my domain, and these souls need me. It's where I belong. I may not have been able to help Pegasus—and his soul is most definitely not here, I've searched for it—but I can come to these unfortunate peoples' aid.

I exhale steadily, then move to the en-trance and step through. Multiple pairs of eyes meet mine. The souls, in their translucent form, shimmer and float. I make my way to the center of the audience hall, where Persephone awaits by my throne.

Whispers increase as I move, and something tightens in my back. Recollections of the past. Of Olympus. But this isn't Olympus. And these souls are not the selfish deities I've lived around. Their whispers are of awe, of excitement, not of shunning.

Persephone's eyes meet mine, and she smiles. I don't have to read her thoughts to feel the pride shining through, the love suffusing her body and our bond. She's been everything I've needed in this adjustment period, and more.

Once I get to the throne, I take a seat and face the crowd of souls. "Welcome to all." My voice reverberates in the hall—I'll have to remember to thank the satyrs for their help. "As some of you may already know, I set up these audiences, which will be open forevermore every week, to ensure you all have a medium within which to communicate with me. Your frustrations, your fears, your hopes... Whatever it is I may help with, voice them now. All I ask is that you do it in an orderly way, one at a time." I survey them all, then point to a frail old man. "Let us begin with you, my friend. What's your name?"

"Barak, my lord." He takes a deep breath, his eyes shining with tears. "I come to you seeking but one thing. My wife. Her name is Amaltheia, and she passed away many years before me, but I have yet to find her. And I have sought her, my lord, sought her for so long."

Persephone's hand is on my shoulder, suffusing me with strength. She knows I still mourn Pegasus' death, and not having full information as to who'd killed him. But I set that aside, instead focusing on the soul. There will be time for answer seeking later.

"Barak, I'll do my best to help."

I get up and move closer to him. He seems so frail, I practically tower him. I hold out my hand, and he reaches for it. All those of the Underworld can touch each other, and it seems the moment I proclaimed myself Lord, that particular gift became mine, and Persephone's as well. It also extends to the satyrs, which will come in handy for unruly souls.

When my hand touches Barak's, I'm jolted into his mind, into his memories. Of the time of his marriage, his first fight, his first newborn. Their new house. His wife's smile. I focus on that energy, on the love that shines between them.

I open my eyes, back in the present.

Barak is trembling. *If he can't help me, I don't know what I will do. I'm already dead, but this feels like dying all over again without her.*

I reach into the air, the web of which parts and lets my hand into nothingness. Into the very web of the matter that has created this realm, the very thing that decides where everything is. And as I reach there, I focus on Amaltheia's face and call to her. With my mind, with my very being, I focus on her…

And then there's a gasp. I open my eyes once more. A new orb is floating in the air above us. Its silvery shine reflects light everywhere, before stopping right in front of Barak's face. His trembling ceases, as if he's already felt her.

And sure enough, a moment later, the orb lingers closer to the floor, and elongates, becoming a woman. Rather, the soul of a woman.

"Amaltheia!" Barak cries, pulling her into his arms.

I close the opening I'd created, the one into nothingness, and turn to Persephone. Pride shines in her eyes, and lifts my spirits higher than I'd ever thought. With measured footsteps, she ushers the reunited couple to the side, making way for the rest of the souls.

A different energy runs through the room now, filled with something I've never had.

Respect.

I have had shunning, and awe, and fascination, and curiosity, and all kinds thrown at me. But respect… I bask in the feel of it for a moment, then gesture to the next soul, a little girl.

These are my people, and this...is where I finally belong. No longer hiding in the shadows, but front and center, leading in my own way.

With kindness and respect.

EPILOGUE

Eons later...

The sound of my footsteps is loud, too loud as I rush to make the audience hall. Ileana didn't give me enough warning, but then again, the fault does not lie with her. I would have stayed behind, even if I'd had more time, because I needed to make sure Persephone would be protected. I cannot risk her, not now, not ever. I will not be responsible for another Olympian's death.

I reach the doors, pausing. So long ago, I was exiled here. It had been the best thing to happen to me. And then the fight landed at my doorstep. Was it one particular thing? No. It was many. But the last thing, the one drop that toppled the vase, was one zmeu's desire to overthrow the old order. To get revenge for centuries of wrongdoing at the hands of immortals, and his own brother.

Unfortunately, he didn't realize the extent of his mistake until it was too late.

And now we will all pay, unless we work together.

Zeus' voice echoes from within, ominous with accusation and withheld contempt. "I asked a question, and I demand an answer."

That, more than anything, gets me moving. I push the doors open and walk in.

The vast hall stretches before me like a mausoleum. Thick Greek columns on each side support a domed archway. Gold litters the floor, moving and slithering through the white marble as if it's alive. A deadly silence reigns in the gathered audience. And in the centre, facing Zeus himself, are my old guardians, their backs to me.

Zeus' eyes narrow on me. "Hades? I take it you cleaned up your Underworld without my help, then?"

I never needed your damned help. I bite down the words, taking a deep breath.

Then I step to Ileana's side, glaring at him. "Not quite, brother. In fact, that is why we are here."

Frumos, silent until then, drops to one knee. Ileana joins him, also kneeling. Only when Zeus gestures for them to say their piece does she speak again.

"Mighty Zeus, we come in peace, and warning. Tartarus has been breached, and all the pantheons are in danger."

Dead silence is replaced by a pandemonium of chaos. Their thoughts assail me, driving me crazy in a familiar way. It has been a while since I have been around such deities, with such power.

Still, I clench my fists, drawing in steady breaths, learning to block them out.

"Enough," I say. My voice, though quiet, reverberates in the mausoleum, and they all fall silent, one by one. "Not many of you will remember that, eons ago, I was banished to the Underworld. I made it my home. I protected Tartarus. And when the Titans broke out weeks ago, I made sure to shove them back in."

Zeus smirks, ready to take credit for that, but I butt in before he has a chance.

"Long ago, you all made the decision to drop your evils in Tartarus. Because they had learned to escape your prisons, and you were starting to lose your grips on them. And I helped. I offered the suggestion to have all the enchantments in one spot. And it worked. For many centuries, for millennia, even, we were safe." I pause, gazing at each god in turn. "Now, it is I who is losing my grip. And unless we all work together, our realms, and the human one, will be destroyed."

A familiar face steps out of the crowd, dressed in green—Morrigan. She promised me that when shit came to shove, I would have her help. And she's here, keeping that promise. "How can we help?"

"We need to neutralize these foes, once and for all!" Thor says. "Enough is enough. They claimed my friend's life long ago."

"No." Shocked eyes turn to me, questions rising in everyone's thoughts. They are not used to me being this in control., but the joke is on them. "Fenrir is not dead. In fact, if I am to believe it, he is very much alive. And that is where our quest begins." I scan their faces, seeking one in particular. "Artemis."

She lifts her head and takes a few steps forward. Her long, fiery hair is braided neatly on her back. Curly tendrils escape, framing a heart-shaped face with freckles. She places the tip of her bow on the shiny floor, waiting.

"You are our huntress," I say. "If I give you a trail, can you track him down?"

"Yes, of course."

I nod, turning to Thor and his pantheon. "We will bring Fenrir to you, once we find him. But that is where it will start."

"Are the Olympians to lead us, then?" Another face emerges from the crowd. Feline ears, green eyes, but human features.

Bastet, goddess of domesticity, women's secrets, fertility. She's part of the Egyptian pantheon but is usually quiet at these gatherings on account of Hera overshadowing her. Deities don't share the spotlight, one could say.

"Mind your mouth, Bastet," Zeus says, not even looking at her. "Of course, we will. When have we not?"

"Perhaps it's time to leave someone else

in charge, since you have fucked us all over so nicely." Her smile is all cat-like.

Morrigan snaps her fingers. "Let us leave all thoughts of overthrowing. At least until Fenrir is found, yes?"

Nods all around. I shoot her a grateful smile.

We have gained time... Until Artemis returns.

Will Artemis' quest lead her to finding wolf god Fenrir? And what secrets lie along the path? What romances may blossom? Find out in the next Immortal Rogues installment, Archer's Arrow.

Available for pre-order today!

To be continued....

And if you enjoyed Hades' story, please consider leaving a review at your choice of retailer. Even a line or two makes a huge difference to an indie author!

Rogues Extended Universe – Reading Order

Moonlight Rogues
Flaming Rogues
Immortal Rogues
Lost Royals of Transylvania
Vârcolac Legacy (coming 2022)

ABOUT THE AUTHOR

Alexa Whitewolf is a fiction writer, newspaper columnist of daily issues and author of the critically acclaimed *Moonlight Rogues* shifter series.

Alexa has been a lifelong writer and first began creating other worlds and characters at the ripe age of 12. Growing up in the Transylvania region surrounded by epic mountains and a never-ending stream of legends and stories was bound to create an overactive imagination. This shines through Ms. Whitewolf's writing by creating worlds filled with unique folklore, life wisdom and plenty of furry creatures.

An avid traveler, Alexa writes under a penname and spends her days between an office job and writing in Canada's capital, when she's not flying somewhere with lush landscapes and plenty of hiking trails.

Her series focus on strong heroines, kind yet sexy men, fights of good and evil and the never-ending learning curve of humanity's strong—and weak—points. Romanian folklore is intertwined with her writing, more notably in her shifter romance series, the Moonlight Rogues. Her other series draw on world mythology, such as the Avalon myth and Arthurian legend (*The Avalon Chronicles*) and Ancient Egypt (*The Sage's Legacy*).

You can follow her blog at www.alexawhitewolf.com/blog or on social media. Her column in Observatorul also tackles various issues, including health, technology, and a writer's life.

If you want up to date releases, make sure you sign up for her newsletter. For new releases notifications, you can also follow her on Amazon and BookBub.

ALSO BY THE AUTHOR

Rogues Extended Universe

Moonlight Rogues series
Moonlight Rogues: Origins
First to Fall
Second to Surrender
Third to Tumble
Last to Love

Flaming Rogues series
Fanning the Flames
Igniting the Ice

Immortal Rogues series
Secret Shadows
Archer's Arrow
Cat's Charms
Trickster's Trap
Fickle Fate

Lost Royals of Transylvania series
Immortal Illusion
Cracked Casualty
Deadly Deceit
Blind Burden
Angry Addiction
Primal Protection

Demoni Sancti Extended Universe

Standalone
Blazing Ashes

Demoni Sancti series
Fallen
Broken
Unshackled
Risen
Ascended

The Avalon Chronicles series
Avalon Dreams
Avalon Wishes
Avalon Nightmares
Atrox

The Sage's Legacy – YA series
The Dragon Medallion
The Dragon Manuscript
Relics of the Underworld

Standalone novels
Blood Ties, Love Binds
Unconditional Love